NATIONAL SERVICE - BOOK TWO OF BEYOND THESE WALLS

A POST-APOCALYPTIC SURVIVAL THRILLER

MICHAEL ROBERTSON

Email: subscribers@michaelrobertson.co.uk

Edited by:

Terri King - http://terri-king.wix.com/editing
And
Pauline Nolet - http://www.paulinenolet.com

Cover Design by Dusty Crosley

National Service - Book two of Beyond These Walls

Michael Robertson
© 2018 Michael Robertson

National Service - Book two of Beyond These Walls is a work of fiction. The characters, incidents, situations, and all dialogue are entirely a product of the author's imagination, or are used fictitiously and are not in any way representative of real people, places or things.

Any resemblance to persons living or dead is entirely coincidental.

All rights reserved

No part of this publication may be reproduced, stored in a retrieval system or transmitted in any form or by any means electronic, mechanical, photocopying, recording or otherwise, without the prior written permission of the author except in the case of brief quotations embodied in critical articles and reviews.

READER GROUP

Join my reader group for all of my latest releases and special offers. You'll also receive these four FREE books. You can unsubscribe at any time. Go to - www.michaelrobertson.co.uk

Michael Robertson

EDEN

A Short Story About The Zombie Apocalypse

RAT RUN

A POST-APOCALYPTIC TALE

Michael Robertson

CHAPTER 1

Butterflies danced in Spike's stomach as he headed towards the gates with his team. A nod at Max, he said, "Good luck, man."

They shook hands, and Max pulled a tight-lipped smile.

"Is it going to be like this for the next five months?" Olga said.

When no one replied, she pointed at Spike and Max. "These two being overly polite to one another to cover up how desperate they are to win the place on the trials."

"You don't seem very worried about what lies ahead," Max said.

She shrugged. "What will be, will be. Although, you two are lucky I don't want to be the next protector; you'd be consoling one another for missing out rather than slapping each other's backs and being jolly good sportsmen."

Olga always made Spike smile, but the smile dropped the second he looked at the gates.

"And to think you nearly died on the first day, Spike."

It was like she'd read his mind.

"Were it not for Ore's crossbow skills, Max would have a much easier run at this."

"Thanks for reminding me."

"You're welcome."

As he returned his focus to the gate, Spike filled his lungs with the fresh spring air. Someone had lined up supplies for the cadets: wheelbarrows, buckets, and tools—most of it made sense: bricks and rocks for building the walls, tools for digging mud from the ground, but … "Why's there loads of dry grass there?"

Hugh spoke for the first time that morning. "They mix it with the clay and water. It helps bind the walls." Although he put his focus on the ground, he stole a quick glance at Elizabeth.

"I always wondered where we sent all the grass from the agricultural district," Spike said.

The slight brown tinge to Hugh's skin had turned almost green, his brow glistening with sweat. After patting his back, Spike said, "We'll be okay out there. I promise."

"You can't promise that, but thanks for saying it." The boy returned his focus to the ground. He held his jaw with a tight clench, and his nostrils flared as he breathed.

To watch Hugh's breathing quicken and his eyes spread wide gave Spike the warning he needed to jump aside, clattering into Max as Hugh threw up his breakfast.

Although they all stopped and Elizabeth leaned down towards Hugh to rub his back, Bleach waved them on. "Get to the gates," he said before he put his arm around Hugh, who vomited for a second time. "I can't believe we're only a month in. Five more months of this before I get *any* time off."

Team Minotaur arrived at the gates and lined up by their supplies. Dragon stood on their left. It caught Spike off guard when Matilda looked back at him and smiled, her hair tied up with his mum's hummingbird clip. She'd spent the past month ignoring him, and although they'd resolved their issues, the fear of rejection still tugged at his confidence.

They lined up much like they sat in the dining hall. It put team Bigfoot next to Dragon. Although, for the first time since they'd started national service, Ranger didn't try to talk to Matilda. From the downturn of Lance's bottom lip, it looked like he hadn't made an effort with him either. His heavy brow hooded his dark and unfocused eyes. The hole had clearly done a number on him, robbing him of his cocksure swagger—not that Spike missed the boy's arrogance.

Sarge already stood in front of the gates. Unlike the rookies, he hadn't had to go back to his dorm to get weapons. The man rarely went outside the wall, but Spike would never ask why. Many of the leaders had already lined up behind him, and once Bleach delivered Hugh back to his team, he took his place with them.

When Spike patted Hugh's back, the boy offered him a tight-lipped smile, his skin still as pale.

Wearing his usual hard scowl, Sarge took his time surveying the gathered rookies, his top lip arching in a sneer. The gates blocked a lot of the wind's force, but it still had the strength to shake his thick grey hair. "It's May the first, losers. I must admit, I'm surprised we still have forty-two of you left. I expected at least one of you to do something stupid by now. A cadet once burned his dorm down while making toast. It killed him and all of his team. That's why we allow nothing other than beds in the dorms now. But someone normally finds a new and inventive way to put themselves and everyone else in danger. I suppose what I'm trying to say is"—a slight twist to his hard features as if he felt a stab of pain—"well done?" More a question than praise, he let the silence hang for a few seconds. "But don't worry," he said, beaming a wide smile, "you'll be dropping like flies from here on out."

Although Spike noticed Hugh pulling at his collar as if he couldn't breathe, he kept his eyes ahead and stepped away from him. If the boy had anything left to vomit, better he did it now while the gates were still closed.

"The countdown begins today," Sarge said, the sound of his voice echoing across the national service area behind them. "If you hear me tell you it's October, then you've done something right—even if that just means you've been exceptionally lucky. Survival, however you achieve it, is a win."

Come October first, Spike would be lining up for the protectors' apprenticeship trials.

Sarge scanned the faces of the cadets, clearly revelling in the drama. When he got to Hugh, he grinned. He walked over, stopped just a foot in front of him, and sniffed. "You emptied your stomach yet, boy? You ain't got time to puke outside those walls, not when you have to fight for your life. You stop and you're screwed. Your team might be screwed too. So, are you done?"

Hugh bit down on his trembling bottom lip.

Sarge leaned so close to him, his nose almost pressed against his face. "I said—"

"He heard what you said."

As gasps ran through the line of cadets, Sarge straightened his back and glared at Spike. A small spasm twitched just beneath his right eye.

Spike held his stare and pointed at Hugh. "He might not look ready—"

"He doesn't."

"But there's no one I'd rather have outside those gates with me."

A snort of laughter on Spike's left. He made eye contact with Ranger before the slam of Sarge's boot pulled his focus back to him.

Sarge moved so close, Spike smelled his stale breath. He spoke in a low tone. "And who the hell—?"

A roar cut through Sarge's words. Spike turned with everyone to see Magma leading a line of Protectors. Jezebel aloft, he screamed again, a sound without words but filled with meaning. It spoke of courage, fury, and loss. It spoke of war.

While everyone else watched the protectors, Sarge pressed his forehead against the side of Spike's face, his hot breath tickling Spike's inner ear. "You'd best watch yourself, boy." Spinning on his heel, he hobbled back towards the team leaders in front of the gates.

"Thanks, man," Hugh said, his focus still on the ground.

Spike shook his head. "I hate bullies." When he made eye contact with Bleach, he balked at the venom looking back at him. And he couldn't blame him; his first month had been nothing short of disastrous. If he stood any chance of being the next apprentice, he needed to wind his neck in.

Silence swept over the rookies as the protectors moved through them like sated predators who might have one kill left in them. An empty sack hung from each of their belts. Magma had two. The woven fabric might have once been brown, but it had turned black with dried blood. By the end of the day, they'd undoubtedly be bulging with writhing heads and glistening with their spilled essence.

Sarge clapped his hands to get the cadets' attention. "That's right, boys and girls, you have the main protectors going out at the same time as you. On the first and last day, it's just them. From day two onwards, they'll each be taking a team of trainees. One of you will get to join that roster soon enough. I'm sure they need no introduction, but I'll do it anyway."

The protectors walked in front of the gates one at a time.

"Leading the group, the most successful protector ever: Magma."

The cadets erupted, Spike with them. But he looked at Ranger rather than his dad. What would he do if he knew Magma had been the bridesmaid and not the bride? Matilda stared at him, and the skin at the corners of her eyes crunched. She knew what he was thinking. But she also knew he respected her secret.

Sarge shouted to silence the recruits. "They're not performing monkeys; show some respect." The bald woman Spike had seen in the square followed Magma.

"Next, we have Crush," Sarge said.

A redheaded man with a thick beard stepped forward. "One of our longest-serving protectors. He might be older than the others, but he's no less deadly: Rayne."

A mountain of a man with dark hair and dark skin lifted his chin and looked down at the cadets. A furnace burned in his glare. "The dark destroyer: Fire."

The polar opposite of Fire, pasty and covered in scars, a slim and wiry woman who looked like she'd squirm free of any hold was next. "Tougher than gristle and slipperier than an eel in lard: Axle."

The biggest one by far, he even made Crush look small. "This man can turn over buildings: Hulk."

The last one had an athletic build; slim and toned, he looked strong and fast. "The man who's so quick, he's burying a knife between the diseased's shoulder blades before they've even thought about going for him: Warrior."

With the seven protectors lined up behind him and the team leaders, Sarge pointed at the trainees. "Watch these men and women. They're here because they're survivors. They each have their own methods, but the one thing they have in common is their methods work. You'll follow this lot and their teams out every day. They walk through the gates first, minimise the threat of lurkers who are hoping to get a free meal, and make it safe for you to follow behind. Once they've gone from sight, you're on your own."

Pointing at the assortment of building materials, Sarge said, "Three barrows and three buckets for each team. When your supplies run out, there will be more waiting outside the gates."

Spike already stood in front of a wheelbarrow, which he lifted by the handles while watching the protectors turn to the large wooden gates. The tall barrier creaked and groaned against the onslaught from the strong winds outside.

The team leaders stood in front of their teams. They copied the protectors by turning their backs on the cadets.

Letting his wheelbarrow down again, Spike reached over and touched the handle of his broadsword. He could reach it should he need to.

Hugh leaned close. "I've serviced all the weapons."

"You *what?*"

"I asked Bleach, and he said it was okay. I've serviced them all. Sharpened them, tightened them up. I've made them as good as they can be in case we need them."

"In case?"

The slight whine to Hugh's voice made it sound like a plea. "Let me at least hope we won't."

Other than the occasional clearing of a throat, or shifting of bricks in a barrow, near silence hung in the air. All eyes were on Magma. Then a deep heave broke the stillness. Seconds later, the wet rush of vomit hit the ground.

Some of it splashed up Spike's right leg. Apparently, Hugh still had some breakfast in his stomach.

While wiping his mouth with the back of his sleeve, his arm shaking, Hugh kept his head bowed and mumbled, "Sorry."

Ranger snorted another derisive laugh, but before Spike could say anything, Sarge spoke. "You sure you want to go into battle with him beside you?"

"Never surer."

A twisted sneer, Sarge stared at Hugh and shook his head. "Then you're a *fool*, boy. And you're as good as dead."

Spike lifted the barrow again and pulled his shoulders back. He felt Bleach looking at him. He knew when to keep his mouth shut.

"When you're outside those gates," Sarge said, "you need to look after yourself first. If there are only a few diseased, you fight them. If there's any chance of being outnumbered, you run and regroup. The guards on the gates will watch, ready to come out and fight beside you or let you back in. If one person's in danger, leave them. We need to keep our numbers up, so we'd rather lose one of you than several. There's no room for heroes out there."

While listening to him, Spike fought against his natural response to shake his head. Was Sarge insane? He'd fight for his friends if they needed him. Besides, if they brought an army of diseased to the gates with them, there was no way the guards would let them back in. But he kept his mouth shut. As did everyone else.

A moment's pause to see if any of the cadets would respond, Sarge then moved aside.

Magma watched him go, rolling his shoulders and testing his grip on Jezebel. Ranger might be an idiot, but his dad knew about slaying—even for someone who'd come second. The champion protector then raised his weapon, his brothers and sisters on either side of him copying the gesture. Together they roared so loud it damn near shook the gates.

A wild cry replied.

The surrounding tension palpable, Spike noticed tears in Hugh's eyes. He rubbed his friend's back. "You'll be okay, mate, I promise." He looked at Matilda. As much as he wanted to be there to help her, he saw the determined fix to her scowl. She'd be fine. He should be more worried about himself and whether Hugh got them both killed. But it didn't matter what Sarge said, no way would he leave a friend to perish.

The protectors roared again.

The wild and shrill cry outside the walls responded, thuds of bodies crashing into the gates. It didn't matter how many times Spike had thought about this moment, nothing could prepare him for the reality. They were finally going to war.

Jezebel still raised, Magma called, "Open the gates."

Thick chains hung down either side of the gates. When the guards turned their winches, they snapped taut. A second later, the large wooden barriers moved inwards. Spike stared ahead with unblinking eyes and swallowed a dry gulp. His stomach turned backflips as he breathed in the acrid stench of Hugh's vomit.

CHAPTER 2

Spike's pulse quickened when an arm shot through the gap in the gates. Atrophied, pale, and sinewy, the hand bent around at what looked to be an impossible angle. It clawed in the direction of the lined-up protectors. He heard Hugh panting beside him as he chased his breaths as if to catch a panic attack before it caught him.

The hand looked more insect than human. Its fingers twitched with erratic spasms. The snapping grip appeared desperate to grab something other than air. The screams of the diseased beyond the gates grew louder, spurring the reaching hand on. Hugh stepped closer to Spike.

As much as Spike wanted to tell him everything would be okay, the grim set of many of the protectors' faces contradicted that. A loud *bang* then crashed against the other side of the gates, and both Spike and Hugh jumped. The gates leaned forward from the pressure. "Just stay close to me," Spike said. "We'll get through this."

When Hugh didn't reply, Spike looked at his friend. Paler than before, his dark eyes were spread wide. It took for Elizabeth to grip his shoulder to break him out of it. Hugh forced a smile at her and she returned the gesture. "You okay?" she asked.

Hugh nodded.

The screams outside grew in volume. They were frantic and frenzied. The gates opened wider, and a head poked through the gap. Wrinkled skin, blood glistened in its glare. Sticky crimson trails ran down its pallid face. It had a deep tear through its cheek, exposing the white of its jawbone.

Magma stepped forwards, yelled, and threw Jezebel in a wide arc. Not only did it sing, but the blade danced too. It moved through the creature's neck without resistance. Its head hit the ground with a thud.

As it rolled around in the mud and grass, Spike heard the castanet click of its snapping teeth. Magma raised his foot before slamming down a heavy boot on it. A wet crunch silenced the clacking thing.

The gates continued to shake, the tops of them swaying. More arms reached through. The screams and hisses grew louder. The tattoo of thuds against the other side beat like war drums.

"The protectors look worried," Hugh said.

"They can deal with this." Then Spike saw Bleach draw his broadsword.

"You were saying?"

"Bleach is getting ready just in case."

"And you think that's common?"

When Bleach looked to either side of him at the other leaders, all of them followed suit.

While whimpering, Hugh moved so close to Spike, they touched shoulders. "There are too many of them."

Spike moved him away with a gentle nudge. "Come on, hold it together."

Matilda watched the gates like everyone else. A strong set to her jaw, she shifted her weight from side to side as if getting ready to charge. Spike didn't need to worry about her.

Two diseased then burst through. Flailing arms and wild shrieks accompanied their uncoordinated charge.

Another deep roar from Magma. It rang so loud Spike could have sworn he saw the diseased flinch. Two heavy swings and he split the skull of one before decapitating the other.

Hulk stepped forward and stamped on the severed head.

The gates swayed as if under the assault of a hurricane.

"Do you think the hinges will hold?" Hugh said.

"They've held until now."

When Hugh stepped back, Spike grabbed his arm. "Don't," he said. He looked at Elizabeth and Heidi too, extending the order to them.

"But those gates are going to give."

"So be ready to attack. A weak link puts us all at risk."

Although Hugh held his ground, he looked ready to run at any moment.

"Also, trust the protectors. They know what to do. Follow their lead and we'll get through this."

Tears filled Hugh's eyes.

When Spike turned back to the front, he saw Sarge nod at the team leaders. Four of them ran at the gates. Two on each side: Fright and Ore on one gate, Crush and Tank on the other. They matched the force of the diseased, closing the gap down the centre.

But the diseased redoubled their efforts, the gates opening again.

Spike put his wheelbarrow down and checked his sword on his back. "Bleach?"

Their team leader looked back at him, an anxious crease to his brow.

"Can we help?"

He stared at Spike before looking at Sarge. When Sarge gave the nod, Bleach returned it to Spike. "Just be ready."

Spike removed his broadsword with the familiar ring of steel and heard several other cadets do the same, including Max, Ranger, Matilda, and Olga. Another surge of adrenaline dared him to charge, but he held his ground.

Hugh kept his sword sheathed, so Spike said, "The only way to deal with your fear is to confront it."

The mole of a boy drew his weapon and wrapped his two strong hands around the handle. Elizabeth and Heidi copied him.

Despite the growing gap in the gates, the diseased's haste created a bottleneck. A growing wall of ugly and angry faces squeezed into the space and held fast.

Although Spike and several others had taken the initiative to draw their swords, many of the cadets still hadn't. Not that it mattered when Bleach shouted, "Put your weapons away and down your tools."

They were going to retreat? But before Spike could question it, Bleach added, "We need to hold the gates. We need to keep these bastards out."

Spike sheathed his sword as the gap in the gates grew wider still. The leaders on either side were slipping against the force of it. He dragged on Hugh's arm to bring him with him, joining Crush and Tank's side. So close to the diseased, the foetid air overwhelmed his senses and he heaved. His eyes watered as he dug his feet into the muddy ground.

Another strong surge hit the gates, and Spike's feet slipped. He nearly fell. The cadets continued rushing forward, slamming into either side as they tried to take control back.

The bottleneck broke. The diseased burst through. Gritted teeth, Spike pushed with such force against the hard wood it stung his shoulder. The protectors stood before the stream of creatures.

A machine, fluid, unerring, and with deadly accuracy, Magma

took down anything that came close to him. Of all the protectors, he made it look effortless like a well-choreographed dance. Most of the other protectors had jaws set in grim determination as they hacked withered flesh and scythed down the diseased. All except Warrior.

Wide eyes and a rictus grin, Warrior's shrill laugh rang out above the chaos. A long two-handed war hammer in his strong grip, he smashed skull after skull. Several of their heads splayed like tent pegs from the blows driven down on them. Although he moved with less grace, he dropped as many as Magma.

"I'm scared, Spike," Hugh said, his red face sweating. "What if these gates don't hold?"

"We'll make them hold. We have to."

"But there are too many of them."

"It doesn't matter how many there are. If we can keep the gap small enough, the protectors will deal with them."

As Spike said it, the protectors moved back as one. It left a line of fallen diseased between them and their aggressors. Many of the second wave charged through, tripped and fell. It made them easy prey for a sharp point, curved axe, or shattering hammer blow.

But then the diseased stopped. Still plenty on the other side of the gates, the ones in Spike's line of sight parted and pulled away.

Hulk's deep voice filled the silence. "What the hell?"

Before anyone could respond, a diseased moving at a full sprint burst through. It stepped on the fallen bodies and leapt at Warrior.

Everything appeared to move in slow motion. The creature flew through the air and reached out with skinny arms, its bloody mouth spread wide to issue a cry. Warrior wound his hammer back to hit it for a home run. But before he could swing, Magma stepped in between them and split its skull. It halted the beast's momentum mid-flight and slammed it into the ground as it adopted Jezebel's trajectory. Both the battle-axe and the beast ended buried in the now blood-soaked mud.

Warrior stood still and silent, staring at Magma as everyone around them held their breaths—everyone but the diseased, who continued to yell and hiss. Magma had crossed a line in not letting Warrior deal with it on his own. But instead of losing his head like Spike expected him to, Warrior's face lit with glee, and he threw his mouth wide in a booming laugh before he ran at the gap and the remaining diseased. He planted himself on the mound of bodies and let the beasts rush him.

From where Spike stood, all he could see was Warrior's smiling grimace, his swinging arms, and the splash back of red pulp. Tallies didn't matter to him; it was all about the kill.

In that moment, Spike knew he had to be a protector. He needed it in his life as much as he needed Matilda. Despite the effort it took to keep the gates shut, he couldn't help but smile.

CHAPTER 3

It took only seconds for the smile to fall from Spike's face, the need to keep the gates closed pushing aside any pleasure he might have gotten from the show. The fight had lasted longer than he expected, his feet slipping in the mud as he tried to find purchase against the gates.

Warrior remained in the central gap, standing on a pile of corpses while he dispatched the diseased one after the other. Spike's mum always used to tell him to dance like no one was watching; Warrior fought as if no one watched. His face alive, his eyes wide, his teeth clenched—whatever moment he existed in, he looked to be in it alone with the diseased.

Sweat stung Spike's eyes, and he fought against his tight lungs, but the press from the other side didn't allow him to sate his need to regulate his breaths. Despite wanting to watch Warrior, he found it easier to drop his focus to the ground and shift his stance to press his palms against the wood. A deep ache in his shoulders, his arms wobbled under the strain. It took for someone to tap his head for him to look up again.

Bleach stood behind him. "You can let go now, boy."

The protectors had already gone through the gap in the gates.

The pile of dispatched creatures looked to have doubled. How many had Warrior taken down single-handedly? Spike straightened up and winced as he rolled his shoulders. Several twinges ran up the back of his neck. It took a few seconds of searching to see Matilda. A sheen of sweat glossed her olive complexion. He gave her a thumbs up and mouthed, *Are you okay?*

She nodded, her eyes widening ever so slightly, her cheeks puffing as she blew out.

Despite the terror from the hole remaining in his glazed stare, Ranger appeared to have coped with the struggle just fine. He turned his lifeless focus on Spike. It sent a slow chill crawling through him. Some part of the boy had remained in that pit.

Spike rubbed his neck under Bleach's scrutiny. "It's over?"

An uncharacteristic smile, Bleach nodded and patted him on the shoulder. "For now. There will be more; there's always more. Well done for taking the initiative to help us. The extra push from the cadets made all the difference."

So caught up in the moment, Spike only just then saw how few cadets had joined in. He met the eyes of several of them, every one averting their gaze. He'd come here to make a difference; they needed to decide their own purpose.

Once Spike had moved back through the cadets, returning to his wheelbarrow and lifting the handles, Hugh patted him on the back. "Well done."

"Thanks, man. And you too. Good on you for joining in." A look at his other team members, he smiled at Max and Olga, who'd also rushed to the gates.

∼

THE CHAINS RUBBED AGAINST THE WOOD AGAIN AS THE GUARDS returned to their winches. The pyramid of corpses turned into a sprawl with the widening gap. Like with the diseased brought into the city for show, many of the cadavers wore clothes Spike hadn't seen before. Some had uniforms on, but even how their garments had been made looked alien. Certainly nothing like those from the textiles district.

Despite there being more dead diseased than he'd ever seen in his life, Spike didn't look at them for long. Not with the view in front of him. His first chance to see this way out of the city, he looked at the sprawl of lush green grass, much of it flattened from where it had been trodden on so many times. The new wall ran from each side of the city and formed a vast semicircle that ended about one thousand feet away. The wall had many gaps in it from where it had been worked on at different points. About ten feet tall, it had stakes planted in the ground along it. It would be high enough to keep the diseased out. Once the gaps had been closed off, they could move the gates, claim the space, and build it higher from the inside. "So this is what Sarge meant when he said it was nearly done." Spike looked at Hugh. "Do you think we'll see the extension completed in this national service?"

If Hugh replied, Spike didn't hear him, his attention drifting to the seven protectors. They'd walked a well-trodden path and were just leaving the perimeter of the new wall. They'd soon be swallowed by the tall grass beyond. They were heading in the direction of what looked to be a ruined city, a lost civilisation of broken towers and crumbling buildings. "One day I'll be exploring that place."

Hugh simply shook his head. "I'll live it through the stories you bring back with you."

The wheelbarrow filled with bricks tugged on Spike's already sore shoulders. Despite the sharp bite in the air, he sweated from the workout, his palms slick against the barrow's handles.

As the first leader to move, Bleach led the way around the fallen, his team following behind while the two guards on the gates moved away from their winches to drag the bodies out into the long grass.

Many of the creatures lay with their mouths open wide as if the last of their life had left them in a scream. The red in their eyes had turned dark from where the blood flow had dried.

Although Bleach didn't turn around, he spoke loudly enough to be heard over the wind. "This was a big horde. Be extra careful out there today. If there's a group like this out in the open, we've got our work cut out."

When Spike looked at Hugh on his right, his frame tight against the constant motion of his heavy water bucket, he saw him scan the landscape. The rest of the team stretched away from him: Elizabeth and Heidi next to Hugh, Max and Olga farther along still.

The same bounce she always had in her step, Olga nodded at the guards piling the bodies. "What happens to them when they're outside?"

Bleach looked at her. "They get taken into the long grass and burned."

"Nice job."

"Hopefully it will make you appreciate yours a bit more."

"I'll get back to you on that. I've not done much digging before."

"You're in for a treat. The clay's nice and thick."

The wind stronger now they'd passed through the gates, Spike tensed against the tipping barrow. Not only did the breeze blow with more force, but the air felt different. It had an earthy, moist smell to it unlike anything he'd experienced in the city—even in the agricultural district, they didn't have the space to let the grass grow like this inside Edin's walls. Every acre of land needed to be put to use and couldn't be left fallow for longer than a season. This meadow looked like it had been left for centuries.

As they got closer to the wall, Spike saw mounds outside the perimeter. Each one had a small cluster of rocks on top. He had to shout to get Bleach's attention, their leader a few steps ahead of them now. "What are they?"

"Burial mounds. Anyone who dies in the city gets buried outside. We can't risk them reanimating, so we bring them out here."

"And I thought our job was bad," Max said.

Bleach smiled. "You should thank your lucky stars you're only lugging bricks."

"And fighting diseased," Olga said, jumping in the air and clicking her heels together in mock celebration.

Hugh whined. "Do you have to be so chipper?"

"When life gives you lemons, Hugh …"

Spike focused on the mounds. It had been a long time since his grandparents passed. He used to go to their house every day after school. They were as much his parents as his mum and dad. "I'm guessing there are a lot of graves?"

Nodding, Bleach spread his arms wide. "They run around the entire length of the wall. Thousands have died over the years, and they're all out here."

Hugh crossed his chest.

Bleach arched and eyebrow and shook his head. "That gesture's all well and good, son, but just make sure you're not one of them, yeah?"

The sound of swishing grass behind Spike accompanied the teams fanning out. Team Yeti, Cyclops, and Chupacabra moved to one side; Dragon, Bigfoot, and Phoenix to the other. They formed a line between them and the city. As if acknowledging the human shield, the sound of chains rushed over wood and the large gates started closing.

For the next few paces, Spike pulled into himself. The hole had helped him be braver, as had the fight in the national service area, but neither could prepare him for this moment. He rolled his shoulders again, feeling the weight of his weapon against his back.

After he'd looked behind, Hugh said, "This is it, then, eh? Well, it's been great knowing you all."

His pulse set off at a canter and Spike shot his friend down. "Shut up, Hugh. We're not going to die. None of us are." He looked at Matilda across the meadow. She had a wheelbarrow too.

"I think it's import—"

"Shut up."

Before Hugh could continue the argument, a diseased's scream called at them from the other side of the wall.

Unsheathing his sword, Bleach kept his eyes forward as he shouted, "Down your tools and draw your weapons." His loud voice carried over the open space as an order to all the cadets.

As Spike lowered the wheelbarrow and drew his broadsword, he did it to the collective ring of steel.

The diseased responded with a hellish cry.

Bleach pulled his sword back as if preparing to swing it. "We have to be ready in case any of them break through. Make sure you hold your ground and let them come to you."

Just one hand holding his sword, Spike kissed his skull ring before gripping on with the other. He looked at Matilda again. The steel in her eyes matched that of the blade in her hand.

No gate to hold the diseased back, Spike focused on the protectors, who formed a line across the widest gap in the wall. They faced the tall swaying grass. While Hugh stood beside him, whimpering, a slight shake ran through his legs. A definitive crack behind them spoke of the gates being bolted. The repeated failures in training flooded back. He had to keep his head. He squeezed his grip even tighter and pulled in a deep breath. It did nothing to ease his tense stomach and pounding heart. Whatever happened, he couldn't afford to fail.

CHAPTER 4

His attention on the seven protectors ahead of them, Spike's legs weakened and his head spun. But he didn't need to worry; nothing would get past them. What had happened in training didn't matter, only how he reacted now. The hole had changed him for the better.

In an attempt to copy his hero, Spike twisted his feet into the trampled grass and gripped his weapon with both hands. Magma held onto Jezebel like he could shatter stone with her. Many of the cadets on either side of him also looked ready, Matilda as set as anyone. Were it not for Artan making her opt out, she'd win the trials hands down. Ranger stood close to her, a spitting image of his dad. A low centre of gravity, he held coiled power in his thick mass. Although, unlike his dad, Ranger looked far from ready for this. The torment from the hole sat in his dark wince.

At that moment, Ranger looked at Spike as if he could hear his thoughts. Spike flinched, the boy's glare coinciding with the next diseased's scream as if he were somehow linked to them. He then gasped to watch Ranger drop his weapon, turn his back on the protectors, and sprint with all he had towards the gate.

"What the—?" Olga said.

A look at the other rookies showed Spike they watched Ranger like he had. They even continued to stare at him when another scream lit up the air.

As if encouraged by Ranger, Hugh stepped back a pace, Heidi and Liz moving with him. Bleach shot them a stern glare and spoke in a low growl. "Hold your place."

Hugh trembled, tears running down his cheeks. He whined and shook his head, but he obeyed their leader. Both Heidi's and Elizabeth's eyes had the same glaze of fear. At least Spike wasn't the only one afraid. He should be nervous. They all should.

All the orders so far had come from Bleach, so Spike jumped at Juggernaut's deep bark. "Eyes front! We'll deal with deserters when this is over. For now, you need to be ready to fight."

Hugh again. "I'm not built for this."

Despite her own struggles, Elizabeth said, "None of us are, sweetie."

Although Spike kept his eyes forward, he felt Hugh visibly relax next to him.

The screams from the long grass grew louder. Suddenly, Warrior broke away from the other protectors.

Although Spike lost sight of him to the long grass and the erected parts of the wall, he tracked Warrior's course through the thuds, cracks, and screams.

A diseased then ran at Hulk. Naked from the waist up, it had once been an overweight woman. Saggy breasts hung down like the protectors' sacks.

A brute of a man, Hulk stood about six feet six inches tall. A sword in each hand, he moved with a grace befitting someone half his size. A flick of his wrist and he speared the diseased through the centre of its face. The creature's legs folded beneath it and it went down.

The next diseased appeared. Although fast, Magma moved quicker, cracking it with the broadside of his axe. Its legs flew up in the air and it landed on its back, out cold. Instead of killing it, Magma pressed his foot against its neck, keeping it pinned. He pushed down with a grimace as if to grind the thing into the mud before he raised his axe again and split the beast's skull.

Six more diseased tore around the corner, the one at the front missing an arm. It hurtled at the protectors, face first, its gait twisted forwards due to its absent appendage.

The protectors dispatched them with minimal effort.

Several more of the wretched things appeared. One of them got too close to Hulk, who abandoned his grace and punched the thing out cold before Axle finished it off. It almost made Spike smile. But on the other side of the gates, mirth didn't come easily. Also, what would he have done in that situation? If a diseased got that close to him, he wouldn't have the strength to knock it unconscious. But he'd be okay. He'd have to be.

Although Bleach had told his team to hold their ground, Hugh, Elizabeth, and Heidi had stepped back another pace. Above the screams of the diseased, Spike heard Ranger banging against the gates and pleading to be let back in.

While everyone watched the protectors in the full flow of battle, one of the pallid beasts burst through one of the smaller gaps in the wall. What used to be a bear of a man, the disease had withered its mighty frame. Several cadets screamed, and Spike's blood turned cold. He'd faced diseased before, but not like this. Not ones with teeth. Not ones this large. There were no second chances now.

But it didn't head for team Minotaur; the creature ran straight for the yellow tracksuits of Phoenix. Maybe the colour attracted it. Spike's heart sank; Team Dragon was next to Phoenix. But Matilda looked ready.

Spike moved forward a step, and Bleach's arm shot across him. "Hold your ground. Phoenix need to deal with this. We don't need any heroes out here. Heroes get themselves—"

At that moment, Freddie Mac—the most capable of all team Phoenix's cadets—raised his broadsword, let out a scream to match that of the creature's, and charged the thing.

It happened so fast, Spike almost lost track of it. The creature dodged Freddie's clumsy swing before crashing into him. It knocked them both to the ground, Freddie losing his broadsword as they fell. It took for Gauze to yell, "Hold your ground," before Spike saw Ya Supreme rush to his friend's aid.

Spike checked Matilda. His muscles twitched with the need to be beside her. Bleach raised his arm higher as if he could read his mind. One of the few cadets not screaming, Matilda would cope.

Freddie Mac had been taken down just a few feet from team Phoenix. Ya descended on them. The beast bit Freddie's throat, a bloody chunk falling from its mouth as it jumped up and charged.

A moment of hesitation snapped through Ya, his legs betraying him as they buckled and almost gave out. The difference between life and death. The diseased didn't hesitate. It took Ya down like it had Freddie. Ya's defence proved as ineffective, the creature's attack as deadly.

Gauze—red-faced—turned to the remaining four members of his team. He had to shout to be heard over the now crying cadets. "Hold your position. We need to face them as a unit." He spun back around in time for Freddie to reanimate. A dark red hole in the centre of his throat, his eyes leaked blood like crimson wax. He charged Phoenix.

Despite his wounds, Freddie moved fast, catching up to the diseased so they both hit Gauze at the same time. Although the team leader killed Freddie, the original diseased bit into Gauze like it had the other two. The protectors were closing in on Phoenix at a charge.

But even Warrior—driven by his bloodlust and running faster than the others—couldn't get there in time. Gauze reanimated quicker than Freddie had, he and the tall diseased making light work of Flight Stingray, Elysium Cooch, Annabelle Jones, and Marie Strength. Bricks spilled from the wheelbarrows, the buckets of water turned over. The inexperienced cadets stood no chance.

Spike moved forward a step, and Bleach restrained him again. He glared at his leader before looking at Matilda. The chaos was too close to her.

"*This* is your team," Bleach said. "The protectors have got this."

Team Dragon stood ready, tears running down the cheeks of the more fearful members. Unlike Phoenix, they held their ground, Tank keeping them in formation so they could defend as one.

Warrior caught up to Ya and yelled a war cry, raising his hammer as the cadet twitched on the ground. He ended him with a crunch before he could get to his feet. Without breaking stride, the hammer-wielding protector smashed the diseased that had started it all with the upswing of his weapon.

The other protectors caught up, and they went to work on the twitching and reanimating team Phoenix. It pulled the fight away from Dragon. The threat got extinguished with a cacophony of cracks and squelches.

∼

While the protectors took all the diseased down and double-checked they were dead, many of the cadets around them sobbed, some of them wailing at the savage loss of an entire team. Like many others, Spike stood with his jaw open as he watched on.

"It all happened so fast," Hugh said, his eyes lacking focus as he stared into the middle distance.

Bleach snapped at the boy. "It does. It's why you need to listen to orders."

Hugh physically shrank from the berating.

Magma—panting from the effort of what he'd just been through—looked at the gates and watched his son for a moment. They opened, a guard's arm reaching out to pull the boy in. A wince broke his stern glare as he watched the gates close. Tears stood in his eyes. Spike couldn't tell if they came from rage or regret, and when he shouted, his shaking voice still offered no further insight. "This is no place for heroes. We've just lost a team because two *idiots* didn't follow orders. You kids have a lot to learn if you want to make it past the first month."

Bleach raised an eyebrow at Spike. But Spike wouldn't apologise for wanting to keep Matilda safe. He'd try again and with more force if he really had to. He'd also found out he had it in him. Unlike Ranger, he wanted to attack. He'd get through this—whatever it took.

Magma led the protectors away, Jezebel over his shoulder as he walked in the direction of the ruined city.

While looking at the team leaders on either side of him, Bleach blew out, his cheeks bulging. After nodding at them, he addressed the cadets. "Now let this be a lesson to you. We need to get to work on this wall. Someone pick up the bricks and tools team Phoenix have dropped. Dragon, take their bodies to the fire pits in the long grass." He then led the march towards the wall, the teams on either side of them breaking off to work on their own sections.

"We're screwed," Hugh said.

But Spike didn't agree. The wind had been taken from his lungs to see the massacre, but that wouldn't happen to him. He wouldn't let it happen to Matilda either—regardless of their orders.

CHAPTER 5

The tips of Spike's fingers and his palms buzzed with the hundreds of small cuts that had opened up on them. He breathed through the pain as he stacked another brick in the wall. Beside him, Hugh mixed clay, dried grass, and water into a thick paste.

The mixture burned Spike's hands almost as much as the rough bricks and rocks, stinging the wounds already there. But he did his job, picking up another handful and packing it into the spaces, as well as spreading a new layer to bed down the next row of the wall.

Because Spike had his focus on building, he crouched with his back to the long grass and ruined city, placing his trust in the others to protect him. The gates to get back into Edin felt miles away should they need to run.

Another hard gust of wind knocked Spike forward onto his knees. After a life shielded by the wall, exposure to the elements would take some getting used to.

The rest of Spike's team had their own jobs. Olga dug a hole, keeping Hugh supplied with clay. The holes also served as the next batch of graves for Edin's citizens. Max, Heidi, and Elizabeth stood guard, watching the long grass for signs of the diseased. Bleach hovered between the two groups.

While looking at his hands, Spike opened and closed them before calling to Bleach, "It's gotta be time to switch now, surely?"

From what Spike knew of his team leader, he'd expected him to talk more. Being their first day outside the walls, he thought he'd offer more encouragement and guidance. And maybe he would have, but since Phoenix had fallen that morning, none of them had much to say. Although, Bleach did nod in response, signalling they should swap around.

Spike groaned through the aches of getting to his feet, a sharp pain at the base of his back. Despite the glares from Max, Heidi, and Elizabeth, he knew them for what they were and didn't take it personally. Building the wall sucked.

With Bleach on his right, Hugh and Olga on his left, Spike drew his sword and looked over the tall grass at the ruined city about a mile away. The lay of the land blocked everything other than the tallest structures and one hill. It stood out as a prominent feature, the top of it littered with sprawling dereliction. "I can't believe how tired I feel after just one day," he said.

Although Spike looked at Bleach, Olga replied to him, "You should try digging holes for as long as I did."

Hugh replied this time, "It looked like hard work."

The conversation died and Spike continued to look out over the meadow at the devastated city. He filled his lungs, the rich damp aroma of grass riding the strong wind. Even though they were a crumbling mess, a lot of the buildings were still taller than any in Edin. The city spread wider than he'd first thought, and he had no idea how far back it went. "Bleach?"

His team leader looked at him.

"Have you ever been in those ruins?"

The wind didn't discriminate, tossing Bleach's thick brown

hair as he squinted into the distance. For a moment, Spike thought he'd remain mute, but instead he shook his head. "No."

Olga snorted a laugh. "Good chat."

Before anyone else could comment, the shriek of diseased burst from the meadow. Spike's pulse quickened and he lowered his stance. His attention fixed on the grass, he saw Bleach in his peripheral vision show a hand to those working on the wall. "Stay there and let us deal with it. Your job is to build. We'll shout if we need you."

The end of Hugh's sword shook as he held it out in front of him. Olga looked ready, her confidence unwavering.

Another cry and the sound of rushing grass told Spike they were close, but he couldn't yet see where they were in the swaying meadow. Then he caught it. Just a few feet from where they stood, something disturbed the natural rhythm.

Two diseased appeared a second later, and Bleach shouted, "Hold your ground! Let them come to you!"

Spike fought against his weakening grip and pulled his sword back. He stared at the beast closest to him. In his peripheral vision, he saw Bleach step aside to let them deal with it. His throat dry, his pulse rapid, he yelled and swung his sword.

The weight of Spike's weapon drove it through the creature's skull, shearing a slice of its head off and exposing its brain, but the beast kept coming.

Its legs now bandy, Spike jumped aside and watched it fall, face first, against the ground. Before it got up again, he pulled back and kicked its head, his foot burying into the wet mush of the thing's brain. The moist squelch and the toe of his boot sinking to the laces turned his stomach, but it stilled the creature. He looked to see Olga take down the second one with a kick before she drove the tip of her blade through its face. When she'd finished—panting from the effort—she lifted her head. Only then did Spike notice the other cadets—at least the ones he could see

—were all watching, many of them pale-faced and open-mouthed. Including Hugh.

"Hugh!" Bleach said.

The boy turned to their team leader.

"See that patch in the long grass?"

After looking where Bleach pointed, Hugh nodded.

"Take the bodies and dump them there. They'll get burned later."

An argument rose and died on Hugh's features before he sheathed his sword, grabbed the collars of both diseased, and dragged them to where he'd been instructed to go. The two beasts were once women, so they were lighter and easier to move than some might have been.

After Hugh had disappeared into the grass, Spike said, "So what's the story about it?"

Both Bleach and Olga looked at him.

"The city. Who used to live there? Where are they now?"

"The old world's gone, William. What it used to be is neither here nor there. What matters is now. And right now, you need to keep your mouth shut and your eyes peeled for more diseased. They normally only come in ones and twos, so we should be fine, but we don't want anyone else dying today if we can avoid it."

The cuts on Spike's hands stung more than before, his palms sweaty against the grip of his sword. He wiped them on his trouser leg, the coarse fabric intensifying the buzzing burn. If anything, he'd just rubbed the clay and sweat in deeper. Then he saw something, and from Olga's gasp beside him, she must have seen it too.

Before Spike could tell him, Bleach said, "The protectors are back. Sometimes we go in before them, but never after." A louder voice, he called to Max, Elizabeth, and Heidi, "Time to pack the tools up; we're done for the day."

Although Heidi didn't speak, Spike noticed her face relax as she stepped from the large hole. Digging a grave in such a tenuous situation carried a grim weight.

Hugh exited the long grass as the line of protectors drew closer. All seven of them had returned as one. That would be Spike one day. Then he wouldn't need to ask Bleach about the ruined city. Maybe he'd also learn a bit about the place. The sprawling mess had a rich story to tell.

Spike joined Olga and Hugh in helping the others with their tools. Where he'd wheeled the barrow out, Hugh wheeled it back. Spike took the empty water bucket.

With the protectors even closer, Spike now saw the sacks strapped to their belts. They were bulging, writhing, and glistening with freshly spilled blood. The creatures' attempts to bite through the thick fabric were futile, but it didn't look like they tried any less. Five of the seven protectors' sacks were half full. Warrior carried a head by its hair because he didn't have any space left, and both of Magma's were stretched to bursting. Every protector wore blood-soaked clothes. They looked tired, but no less able to fight. They were machines.

Bleach led his team back towards the national service area. For the first time in several hours, Spike saw all of the other teams, many of the cadets walking with tired slumps. From what he could see, Matilda looked to have coped just fine.

As the protectors entered the new wall's perimeter, Spike watched Magma look at team Bigfoot. His usual scowl hooded his searching eyes. Hard to tell, but it looked like a slight sag to his frame when he didn't see his boy.

"Ranger's still not returned," Hugh said.

At that moment, Magma fixed on Spike, his brow dipping lower, his jaw tightening. Spike dropped his focus to the ground. "I think he heard you."

"*What?* He couldn't have."

"Well, he just looked at me like I said it." Another glance at Magma showed Spike the thickset protector still stared at him.

A slight whine lifted the pitch of Hugh's words. "I'm sorry. Shall I say something to him? That it was me? That I didn't mean to say it?"

"*No*, that'll only make it worse. Maybe he didn't hear you. Maybe he just saw me looking at him."

The same rage met Spike when he turned to Magma again. The same rage he'd been on the receiving end of from his precocious son too many times to count.

It took for the sound of a horn to pull Spike's focus back to the gates. Fright—team Chupacabra's leader—had reached them first and signalled they needed to be let back in. Each team leader had a similar horn, as did the protectors; it was the best way to communicate with the guards from outside the wall.

The familiar sound of chains rushed over wood as the gates shook and wobbled. A few seconds later, a gap split down the middle. Spike strained to listen for the distant call of diseased in case they'd heard the horn. Nothing. Magma might have been staring daggers into his back, but there was no other protector he'd rather have behind him if the diseased did turn up.

The teams bunched up and waited for the gates to open, the cadets queuing to get back in, the protectors stopping behind them. It took all Spike had to not turn around again. But what would he do? Talk to Magma? Try to awkwardly explain why he'd looked at him? The man probably just wanted to check on his son and go home for the day.

Instead, Spike looked at Matilda, mud on her face, the hummingbird clip in her hair. She looked back at him and raised her eyebrows. He mouthed, *You okay?*

It banished Magma from his thoughts when she smiled and nodded. The broad protector then crashed into the back of him, barging him aside and sending him stumbling forward as he pushed through the crowd to enter the city before many of the cadets.

"Guess he must have heard me," Hugh said. "Sorry."

Because he had nothing positive to say, Spike didn't reply. Day one and he'd seen a team killed, and now his hero hated him. What a start!

"Spike?" Hugh said.

"Sorry, it's been a long day. All I want to do is go back to the dorm and sleep. If this is day one, I don't know how I'm going to feel at the end of five months."

Hugh set off, the wheel on his barrow squeaking. Spike fought through his lethargy and followed him. How many steps would it take to get him from his current position to his bed?

But before he got carried away with thoughts of sleep, Spike heard the gruff clearing of a throat.

Sarge strode in front of them. He waited for everyone to enter and for the sounds of the chains to start up again to signal the gates closing before he said, "We all need to go to the dining hall so we can talk about what happened today."

Although no one protested, Spike noticed many of the cadets around him sag in response to the order. As he watched the protectors walk off in a different direction, he exhaled hard and joined the others in following Sarge towards the dining hall. His bed would have to wait.

CHAPTER 6

The second Spike stepped into the dining hall with his team, he saw Ranger already at Bigfoot's table, and his chest tightened. The same scowling demeanour he'd worn since the hole. Whatever went through his mind, Spike didn't want to know. If only the tragedy that took Phoenix down had taken him with them.

Much of the subdued chatter on the way there died down when the other cadets noticed the boy. They brought in the reek of mud and sweat as they took their seats.

Dark bags sat beneath Ranger's eyes as if the chaos inside his mind ran him ragged. He'd always been a sadist, but he now looked like he wanted to set the world alight just to watch it burn. Not even Lance got a reaction from him as he took his usual seat on his left.

Whereas Ranger had watched Spike all the way to his table, he now turned his attention to Matilda.

The need to scream rose and died in Spike. While chewing on his tongue, he studied the deep pools of hatred in Ranger's eyes. No longer someone who wanted to flirt, the stocky psychopath emanated violence.

When Matilda returned his glare with interest and then flipped him the bird, Ranger dropped his attention to the floor. She could look after herself, but something about the shame on the boy's reddened face sent a shudder through him. Someone who cut that deep would seek revenge.

The rest of team Minotaur took their seats, choosing the same spots they'd had for the past month. Despite the smell of dirty and hard-worked bodies, Spike's stomach rumbled because of the aroma coming from the kitchen. While holding his belly, he turned to Hugh. "I'm starv—" He stopped dead because of Hugh's pallid face and followed his line of sight to Ranger.

"Why's he looking at me?"

This time Elizabeth spoke up, reaching across the table and touching Hugh's arm. She said it loud enough for Ranger to hear. "Ignore him. His head isn't right."

Although Hugh looked like he tried to turn away from Ranger, he managed only a few seconds before he looked back at him again.

The sound of Sarge's heavy limp beat against the wooden stage. The remaining six team leaders sat at the long table. Spike's gaze lingered on the unoccupied chair.

Before Sarge spoke, Ranger hissed across the room at Hugh, "You'd best watch your back."

The reaction rose and died in Spike for the second time in as many minutes. Instead of talking to Ranger, he said to Hugh, "I don't know why he's going for you, but just ignore him." His pulse pounding, he clenched his fists. Could he follow his own advice?

"I'm going to wait until you're on your own and hurt you, you little clown. I'm going to torture you like I would a puppy. You have *no* right being here."

Hugh whimpered, and many of the cadets between him and Ranger shifted as if the boy's threats made them uncomfortable. A locked jaw, Spike looked at the top table and made eye contact with Bleach. Although his team leader didn't say anything, he glanced from Spike to Ranger and back to Spike again before giving a gentle shake of his head.

"If you don't die outside the walls, you'll die inside them."

"Ignore the prick," Olga said. "He's got issues."

Although Bleach saw what went on between them, the rest of the team leaders and Sarge seemed oblivious, some of the cadets still weaving through the tables to take their seats. A deep furrow to Sarge's brow, he looked preoccupied with trying to find the right words.

"We lost an entire team today," Sarge then said and snorted an ironic laugh.

The attention of the room went to the man on the stage. If Ranger still looked over, Spike didn't care.

"That's a first. Before I go on, I want to take a moment to honour team Phoenix." Sarge bowed his head, Spike copying him when he saw many of the cadets do the same. "You gave yourself in service to this great city. May your spirits watch over us as we grow and prosper. Know we won't forget you when Edin is liberated from the oppressive control of trying to live in a world where the diseased exist. Know you are the reason we'll get there."

When he'd finished, Sarge looked out over the tables. Regret glazed his faded blue eyes. He scratched his stubble before pulling in a deep breath. "Death happens on national service, although hopefully far fewer in one day than what you've witnessed today. When it does, we need to ask what can we learn? Could we have done anything differently?"

While letting the silence hang, Sarge's chest rose with a deep breath. "Firstly, what we can learn is the importance of staying together. There's a reason your leaders ask you to hold your line and let the diseased come to you. If Freddie had remained with his team, the diseased wouldn't have taken them down so easily.

Ya trying to be a hero made it even worse. Also, you probably saw how Freddie changed instantly while Ya didn't. Ya's wound was superficial. Although both were infected—which is why the diseased moved on to attack someone else—only Freddie received fatal wounds. It seems the closer the injury takes someone to death, the quicker they turn."

"It's as if the body's fight for survival accelerates the effect of the virus," Hugh said. An impulsive reaction, his face flushed red as if he'd only just realised he'd spoken out.

Silence fell over the hall as Sarge fixed on Hugh. "What did you say?"

At first, Spike felt Hugh look at him. A default reaction whenever he got in trouble he didn't know how to get out of. The boy then looked at Ranger, who glared back. It paralysed him, so Spike shoved him and nodded in Sarge's direction. "You might as well say it."

Hugh cleared his throat and his voice shook when he directed his words at the stage. "The virus reacts quicker in a body that's failing, almost as if the fight for survival accelerates the effect of the disease."

After he'd nodded a few times, Sarge said, "Check out brains over there."

"You mean he has a use?" Ranger said.

Hugh flushed red again.

Where Spike had once seen strength in Ranger, he now saw shame. The boy had publicly humiliated Spike about his fear, and now he was experiencing it himself. Not only that, but he'd run away and begged to be let back in on day one. At some point he'd have to face his old man too. If Spike wanted to be the next protector, he had to keep his head down. Ranger couldn't beat him outside the walls, so it looked like he wanted to do it inside. And he wanted to do it through Matilda and Hugh. No way would he jeopardise his future over a petty squabble with an idiot. Instead, he winked at Ranger and smiled.

Lance Cull's loud and deep voice flew at Sarge. "Why don't the diseased eat their victims?"

Despite Lance's lack of etiquette, Sarge acknowledged the question with a slight nod. "They seem driven to infect and nothing else. They can last for several months, rotting as they walk, but from what we can tell, they don't eat. Ever."

"If they only last for a few months, why haven't they all died out?"

Another good question, Sarge winced while pausing as if thinking about how to reply. He pulled on his collar, cleared his throat, and raised a finger in the air. "Make sure you follow these rules. One: stick together. Two: don't try to be a hero like Ya. You'll only succeed in weakening your team. Three: when someone's been bitten, get ready to kill them. No matter who it is. Any questions?"

"Yeah," Olga said beneath her breath, "the same one Ranger's lapdog just asked: why haven't they all died out?"

From the looks thrown her way, it seemed that many of the cadets close to them heard Olga's question. If any of the leaders did, they ignored it.

Spike looked around the room to see Ranger glaring at him again. He looked back at the boy for a few seconds before staring past him at Matilda. Sarge said don't be a hero, but if he saw her in trouble, he'd do whatever it took to save her regardless of the leaders' instructions.

"Right," Sarge said, "now we're in here and the place already stinks of your sweating bodies, you might as well eat before returning to your dorms to wash. I'd imagine you're all exhausted. Because of our sudden drop in numbers, there's more food to go around. So eat up, and think long and hard about how you're going to deal with the next attack. There's very few things in this life you can be certain of, but dealing with scores of diseased on national service is one of them."

Again, Olga spoke for the benefit of those closest to her. "Scores of diseased that are coming from somewhere you don't feel the need to tell us about."

Spike watched team Yeti get up first for dinner. They walked to the hatch between the dining hall and kitchen. Although he felt Ranger's attention still on him, he refused to look at the boy. He'd quieted down, and in his current state, maybe that was all Spike could hope for. Dog-tired from his day, he needed food, a shower, and bed, in that order. Five months of this could damn well kill him. And if it didn't, he had another five-month fight for the apprenticeship.

CHAPTER 7

The near silence they'd eaten their dinner in—vegetable broth again, albeit more on account of them being six cadets and a team leader lighter—continued as they left the hall, the cadets quietly shuffling out. After the day they'd had, words seemed woefully inadequate.

The second Spike exited with his team, he saw Ranger and Lance waiting.

The same vicious twist to his large features, Ranger focused on Hugh. "You won't be here at the end, boy."

A quick check showed Spike the team leaders were still in the hall. "What are you hoping to achieve by going for him?"

Clearly stirred up by the drama, Lance bounced on the spot, his face alive.

"He's a weak link," Ranger said. "The sooner he goes, the safer it will be for the rest of us outside the walls."

Where Spike wanted to swing for the boy, Hugh had the opposite reaction, his shoulders slumping while he dropped his attention to the ground. Elizabeth reached out to comfort him, grabbing one of his large hands.

A twist to his sneer, Ranger shook his head. "We could do

with the diseased taking your girlfriend from us too. You're dead wood. The pair of you."

"They didn't run away earlier," Spike said.

Both Ranger and Lance puffed out their chests, Ranger the mouthpiece for the pair. "What's that supposed to mean?"

A tight twist wound through Spike's already aching back. When he clenched his fists, the small cuts covering his hands burned. "You should deal with the fear you've developed around the diseased."

"And you'd know."

"You were more than willing to point it out to me when I was at my lowest ebb. It took a stint in the hole for me to deal with it. Have you thought about going back for another visit?"

Ranger's dark eyes lost focus as if he'd returned to the hole in his mind. A few seconds later he blinked several times. Many of the cadets had stopped to watch the strange reaction. The boy clearly still had venom racing through his veins, but he didn't seem able to articulate it. Instead, he turned away from team Minotaur and headed back to his dorm, Lance a few steps behind.

"He's lost it," Max said. Some of the other cadets muttered words to the same effect.

Heidi shuddered. "His dark little eyes give me the creeps."

While watching the hunched shoulders of the stocky boy and his tall greasy friend walk away from them, Spike sighed. "Were he anyone but Magma's son, I wouldn't worry. But you know he's got a ticket all the way to the trials. He's a first-class liability, and he's not going away anytime soon."

The silence hung for a second before the cadets moved off; Hugh and Elizabeth led the way, the two of them still holding hands. Just as Spike passed the edge of the hall, someone reached around from behind the wall, grabbed him, and pulled him towards them.

When he saw who it was, Spike said, "Tilly?"

Half smiling, half flushed, she tilted her head back to indicate her intended destination. "Come with me."

"Where?"

But she didn't answer. Instead, she moved along the narrow side of the dining hall while the rest of the cadets headed back to their dorms.

Just before he rounded the next corner after her, Spike looked back at his team. Although Hugh and Elizabeth still appeared to be reeling from Ranger's unprovoked attack, Max, Olga, and Heidi all smiled at him. Max even gave him a thumbs up.

Spike followed Matilda to the side of the dining hall with the large windows looking out over the national service area. A pillar dissected the wall of glass every few feet.

"They're all still in there," Matilda said, pointing through one of the windows. All of the team leaders and Sarge remained on the stage. Without another word, she darted across the first window and hid behind the large pillar on the other side.

A careful eye on the leaders, Spike jogged to catch up to her. "Where are we going?"

Instead of responding, Matilda darted across to the next pillar.

The leaders hadn't yet clocked them, so Spike drew a calming breath and followed her again.

At the second pillar, Matilda spoke. She fought to get her words past her quickened breaths. "If we want privacy, we need to make sure they don't see us."

"And we want privacy?"

Matilda darted across the third and final window.

Some of the leaders were leaving the hall. Juggernaut and Sarge remained. When Bigfoot's leader hugged Sarge, Spike paused to watch before running to Matilda on the other side. "Did you just see that?"

Together they watched the two men pull apart, the tears on Sarge's cheeks catching the light.

"He's normally so shut off," Spike said.

Matilda's eyes narrowed as she watched him. "The job must take its toll. Maybe it's the only way to cope. The amount of people he's known and lost, I'd imagine it would send him nuts if he bottled it all up. Come on." She tugged on Spike's shirt. "Let's get out of here before someone finds us."

The curiosity of an emotional Sarge kept Spike static. But when Matilda set off again, he ran after her.

Faster than him—always faster than him—Spike pushed his tired body to keep up with her, the uneven ground making his feet roll as they closed down on the gym.

Matilda vanished around the side of the larger building. A few seconds later, Spike followed her.

A ladder of wooden rungs ran up the back wall. By the time Spike got to them, Matilda had already climbed several feet up. They led all the way to the pitched roof at least fifteen feet above them. As he watched her climb, his focus more on her athletic form than anything else, he finally said, "What are you doing?"

Matilda didn't even look back when she reached the roof and climbed onto it.

His hands still sore from his day's work, his muscles tired, Spike shook his head before beginning his ascent.

The rungs were surprisingly easy to climb, a slight lip on the top of each one giving Spike something to hold onto. His sure grip helped him combat the stronger winds higher up.

At the top, Spike crawled over to Matilda.

Matilda grabbed Spike's face with both her hands and kissed him, breathing in through her nose as if she drank him in. When she pulled away, her brown eyes sparkled. "I've been waiting to do that."

"You brought me up here so we could kiss?"

"Is that not a good reason?"

"It's a *great* reason."

They kissed again, her taste as sweet as it had been on the factory roof.

Although Matilda had her hair tied up in the hummingbird clip, the wind found the loose strands and tossed them. They weren't quite as high up as the wall, but Spike still had the best view he'd seen of the ruined city so far. He laughed as he looked at it.

"What?"

"Only you would want to climb up somewhere like this."

"It's been driving me nuts. I saw the rungs on the back wall a few weeks ago and have wanted to climb it ever since."

"Like the barn roof when you were eight?"

"Do you *always* have to remind me?"

"It took me nearly an hour to find a ladder to get you down."

"I know. I was the one who was stuck, *remember?*"

Spike laughed, watching the strands of her brown hair again. "I'm pleased you're still wearing the clip." He showed her his skull ring.

"Of course. I've only taken it off to clean it." She then took his hand and traced a heart on his palm.

"When I saw you didn't have it on, I thought you'd given up on me."

"I gave up on hope. But I only took it off during training to clean it." Before he could say anything else, Matilda smiled. "So … Hugh and Liz?"

"Sweet, isn't it?"

"Are they a *thing*?"

"I guess so. They seem closer than before, and she touches him every chance she gets, but he hasn't said anything to me."

"Well, I hope they are. They suit each other."

The weight of what Spike said next tugged on his heart. "But they're from different districts and neither are protector material."

"I'm sure they're aware of that. They'll work it out. They're smart."

"That's very pragmatic of you."

"I'm trying."

"How do you think Artan's getting on?"

Matilda turned away from him, her eyes glazing.

A minute or so passed before Spike said, "So that was weird earlier."

She turned back. "What part?"

"Not team Phoenix; that was *horrific*. It doesn't matter how many times they told us people will die, I didn't expect it to happen so soon."

"And for so many of them to go."

"Right. No, I mean the bit where Lance questioned Sarge."

"I hate to say it, but for a dullard, he asked some astute questions. If the diseased only last a few months, where are the new ones coming from? Surely they should have died out by now. It's not like the few we evict every week can account for how many there are."

Spike thought about Mr. P and his lover.

Matilda sighed. "But maybe we don't need to know. Maybe it's for our own good."

As Spike thought about her words, he looked out at the ruined city again. Higher up than before, he studied the collapsed sprawl. The metal skeletons of old tower blocks, rubble everywhere … bridges broken off and with what looked like thick metal fibres poking from them … the ruins on the top of the hill … "I bet some of the answers are in there."

"And you want to go and look?"

The devastated mess of broken buildings sent a shudder through him. "Doesn't look like the friendliest place, does it?"

"No."

"What do you think used to be on top of that hill?"

"I dunno, but it's the first place I'd go. It looks like it used to be important to the city."

He winked at her. "And it's a chance to climb something."

The creaking of large hinges pulled Spike and Matilda's attention to the gates separating the national service area from the rest of Edin. A guard had opened them to let a horse and cart inside. "No idiot test today, then?" Spike said.

"Even that seems like a long time ago now. So much has happened."

The driver flicked the reins to lead his horses on and passed beneath them. He carried barrels of bricks and water. "It makes my back hurt just looking at that lot."

"Hard graft, isn't it?"

Spike studied the half-built wall outside the gates. "When I first saw it, I thought we might be the ones to see it completed."

"No chance. Maybe the next lot."

At first, Spike looked nowhere in particular, but his gaze soon fell on the arena in the training area. "The ring seems so much smaller from up here." Before Matilda replied, he saw a small wooden building he hadn't seen from the ground. "What's that?"

"Another dorm?"

"For the cadets on the trials?"

The door opened and someone walked out. A girl—not much older than Spike and Matilda—she stretched as if warming up for exercise. "I'd guess so," Matilda said.

When the girl looked their way, both Spike and Matilda fell flat against the wooden roof.

A second of silence, Spike laughed. "That must have looked weird if she just saw us."

"I know, right? Hopefully she's written it off as her imagination. The stress of the trials is already sending her nutty."

Spike's heart beat faster from fear of rejection, but when he reached an arm up and shifted closer to Matilda, he relaxed to feel her pull in next to him.

"You know that means you're going to have to live with Ranger for five months, right?"

"I hadn't thought about that. Even though he's losing the plot, he's guaranteed to be in the trials at the end of this."

"Yep."

"I'll beat him. Although, after my run-in with Magma today …"

"You had a run-in with him?"

"Well, a silent one."

"Sounds *ferocious*."

"It's serious."

"Sorry. Go ahead."

"When he came back from his day, I watched him looking at team Bigfoot for Ranger. He then looked at me, catching me watching him."

"That's a lot of watching."

"It was the *way* he looked at me."

"You could be imagining it."

"Maybe."

It helped when Matilda turned to Spike and kissed his cheek. She led a line of them down the side of his face to his mouth.

They lay back again, any fatigue Spike felt driven away by his filled heart. "Whatever it takes, I'll do it."

"Including letting me fight my own battles?"

Spike sat up, checking to see the cadet in the training area had gone before he turned to Matilda. "What do you mean?"

"If I get in trouble, I want you to leave me. You saw how quickly Phoenix fell today. Freddie and Ya were idiots trying to take the diseased on. I need to know you'll let me fight on my own. That you won't rush in first and think later."

"Why would I do that?"

"Because Artan needs at least one of us. I hope both of us return, but I don't want you risking your life trying to save mine. I can look after myself. Hell, I can probably do it better than you anyway, so I'm sure it won't be a problem, but I need you to let me fight on my own. If my back's against a wall, I don't need to be worrying about Artan's safety. If you're still alive, I know he'll be okay."

Steel sat in her usually soft gaze.

"Look, Spike, I saw you look over at me earlier when the diseased took down Phoenix. I saw how close you were to abandoning your team. I need you to promise me you'll hold your ground."

"You sound like the leaders."

"They know what they're talking about."

Spike watched the training area again, feeling Matilda's attention pressing into the side of his face. "But what if I think it's the right thing to do? What if I see how I can help?"

"There's a reason the team leaders tell us to hold our ground. They're experienced in this."

"They don't always know best."

"*I'm* asking you to hold your ground. To make sure one of us is guaranteed to get back to Artan."

A few seconds passed before Spike said, "Is that why you brought me up here?"

"I wanted to see you. I wanted to kiss you; that's okay, isn't it?"

Spike folded his arms. "Okay, fine."

"You promise?"

"Yep."

"Say it, then."

"It."

"Say *I promise I won't risk my life to save yours.*"

It made him feel physically sick. "I promise I won't risk my life to save yours."

Matilda leaned close and kissed his cheek again. "I love you, Spike Johnson." She then shifted away from him.

After he'd watched her climb backwards off the roof, Spike fell flat and stared up at the grey sky. Had he just made a promise he couldn't keep?

CHAPTER 8

Although the rest of team Minotaur had gotten their breakfast already, Spike waited at the table, claiming he felt sick and needed a moment to wake up.

When Matilda walked in, he got to his feet, Olga raising her eyebrows at him. "Lovesick, right?"

Spike weaved through the dining hall and slipped into the queue behind Matilda. She smiled at him, but her olive skin looked pale, her face drawn. "Are you okay?"

"I pulled the morning shift on the gate."

"Urgh, grim."

"I know, right?"

"We haven't done ours yet."

"Nothing happens, you just have to stand by the gates so the guards can take the night off. Try to avoid the four a.m. shift if you can."

"*Four a.m.?* I didn't even know such a time existed."

"You do an hour and a half and then can't sleep afterwards because the second you close your eyes, you know someone will wake you up. I'd rather have done a stint in the middle of the night. At least I could have gone back to bed." She yawned and shrugged. "Even talking about it makes me tired."

Spike caught her yawn and clenched his jaw to suppress it, his eyes watering.

The next to the hatch, Matilda smiled at the cook on the other side, held her plate out, and watched as the cook put a chunk of rough bread on it. She garnished it with a dollop of jam. A menu didn't exist in this place. You got what you were given, and you ate it or went hungry.

While receiving the same breakfast as Matilda, Spike said, "It's been a few days since we've caught up; wanna check out the gym roof later?"

Paler than usual, Matilda's eyebrows pinched and rose in the middle. "I'm so sorry. It's not that I don't want to. I really enjoyed our last trip up there, but I need to get some rest."

The reply hit Spike square in the chest. He nodded. "I suppose that's the good thing about getting the Saturday night shift on the gates, you get the next day off."

"I'm sorry," Matilda said again. "This first week has been savage. Add guard duty to it and all I want to do is sleep."

"No, it's fine. I'm exhausted too. It's been a long week."

Just before she walked off, Matilda traced the shape of a heart on his forearm.

While watching her, Spike let out a heavy sigh. Maybe he should take her lead. Rest wouldn't be a bad use of his day. Only the first week of national service—they had a long way to go. The more rest he got, the better his chances of survival. And he couldn't deny that to Matilda. Especially as he'd promised he wouldn't help her if she got in trouble.

A warmer and brighter day than the week that had preceded it, the strong sun shone in through the large dining hall windows, heating the space up and dazzling Spike as he headed back to his team's table. The floors were still damp from where they'd been mopped before breakfast, and because they hadn't been in there long, the air smelled of moist wood rather than sweating bodies or food.

Spike slid his plate onto the table as he sat down. Some of his teammates had finished their breakfast, but they all remained. Hugh and Elizabeth sat closer to one another with every passing day. A slight smile at them, he then rolled some of the aches from his shoulders. He opened and closed his hands several times, his palms and fingers flecked with cuts. "If this is just one week, I dread to think what my hands will look like in five months."

More cadets entered the hall, their feet dragging over the wooden floor, their shoulders slumped. Matilda had been right to schedule rest today. They all needed it. "I'm so glad they give us Sundays off. I'm not sure I'd cope if we had to work straight through for five months."

Olga's cheek bulged from where she moved her mouthful aside to speak. "Hopefully we'll get the extra day off at the end of this month too. Our kill count's good, isn't it?"

"As good as anyone's."

"I'd do anything for an extra day off," Olga said.

Max winked at her. "What I'd give right now to have the power to give days off."

Spike laughed when he saw Olga's cheeks redden as she dropped her focus to the table. "I'm not sure I've seen you blush before."

She looked back up and spoke through clenched teeth. "Tell anyone and I'll cut your throat."

The smile still on his face, Spike caught Matilda's eye. She smiled back. In just five months, this would all be over. In less than a year, he'd be living the life of his dreams.

Heidi pushed her plate away and rested her elbows on the table. "I'm just grateful to get through our first week."

Maybe emboldened by having Elizabeth by his side, Hugh

looked across the dining hall at Ranger. "I'm sure you're not the only one."

It seemed impossible that the short and stocky cadet could have heard him over the noise, but the second Hugh said it, Ranger looked up, deep bags beneath his eyes. Spike had thought Matilda looked tired until he'd seen him. A hard twist to his features, he damn near spat the words across the hall, the room quieting down at the outburst. "What are you looking at?"

When Hugh didn't reply, Ranger stood up. Juggernaut immediately called down at him from the top table, "Sit *down*, Ranger."

The quiet dropped to silence, all eyes turning on Magma's son. He shook his head and pointed at Hugh. "I think this wise arse has something he wants to say to me. Do you have something to say, boy? Do you want to call me out for what happened the other day? Do you want to mock me for running back to the gates? You've no *idea* what I've seen. You don't know what it's like down there."

"Spike does," Olga said, but Ranger ignored her, keeping his attention on Hugh.

Spike watched Hugh's face redden. He then looked at Bleach. Although his team leader had told him to hold back when it came to fighting the diseased, he hadn't said anything about sticking up for teammates when it came to other cadets. He said, "Leave it out, Ranger."

"I wasn't talking to *you!*"

"I don't care. *I'm* talking to you."

Bleach's expression remained unchanged. Spike took it as his approval.

The boys glared at one another while Juggernaut said, "*Ranger!* Sit down!"

But Ranger ignored him and pointed at Hugh again. "He said something about me, and I want to know what it was."

Lance stood up next to his friend as a show of solidarity.

"*Lance,*" Juggernaut said. "Behave!"

Lance sat back down again.

When Spike saw Ranger reach for his butter knife, his entire body tensed. Not the sharpest weapon, but it would do enough damage.

Suddenly Ranger burst to life, roaring as he jumped on his table. He ran over the tops of the three separating them. Fortunately, he dropped the knife in his haste, but he continued to charge. The slam of his boots hit the wooden tops. Plates smashed when he knocked them to the floor.

Spike sat between Ranger and Hugh, so when Magma's son leapt, he jumped to his feet and blocked him, shoving him with both hands.

Ranger fell backwards, his shoulder hitting a bench on his way to the floor.

As Spike positioned himself in front of Hugh—his fists raised—he heard the sound of scraping chairs on the main stage. The thunder of the leaders' footsteps beat a stampede towards them. He noticed Lance descending on them too.

But the team leaders weren't quick enough to stop Ranger getting to his feet and lunging at Spike.

White light flashed through Spike's vision from Ranger's blow. His ears rang and his world tilted. The boy might be a coward, but he hit like a bull.

Before Spike got his bearings, Max and Olga leaped on Ranger, pulling his arms and dragging him down again.

Ranger threw them both off, Olga cracking into team Yeti's table and Max falling to the floor.

Ore reached Ranger first. She hit him hard, landing on top of him as they fell. Her movements turned into a blur, and before Spike tracked them, she had the boy's arm halfway up his back, forcing his cheek against the floor. She leaned close to his ear, spittle spraying from her mouth, her voice echoing through the hall, "We don't tolerate that kind of bullshit here! It's bad enough with those *things* outside the walls."

The rest of the team leaders caught up to her. Tank and Juggernaut grabbed one of Ranger's arms each and dragged him to his feet. The boy shook and twisted in an attempt to get free, his cheek cut from where he'd been pushed against the floorboards. As they led him from the hall, past team Minotaur's table, he spat at Hugh, missing by only a few inches. "This ain't over yet. No one gets away with mugging off Ranger Hopkins. No one."

Like most of the cadets there, Spike watched the writhing Ranger as they led him from the hall. His ears continued to ring and his face stung from where the boy had hit him.

Olga moved back to her table with a slight limp and sat down.

"Are you okay?" Max said.

While nodding, Olga said, "I will be by tomorrow. What do you think they're going to do with him?"

A shake running through him, Hugh rubbed his face. His words were possessed with the same tremble. "Hopefully kick him out. He's a liability. At the very least, they need to make sure he's not allowed to be the next apprentice."

Where Lance had been emboldened by his friend's aggression, he looked to be equally deflated by his exit. Halfway between his table and Minotaur's, he moved back to where he'd come from. Spike watched him all the way. "I think if it was anyone else, they'd already be excluded from the apprenticeship. But he's Magma's son, so they'll give him much more rope."

Hugh used his sleeve to wipe Ranger's spit from the table. "Hopefully he'll use it to hang himself."

CHAPTER 9

The now familiar sound of chains passing over wood triggered a rush of adrenaline, which Spike did his best to contain. When the gap opened by about a foot, the scream of a diseased entered the complex moments before the creature did. As skinny as any he'd seen, it wore trousers and a ripped shirt. It met Axle's wrath. She swung her sword in a wide arc and cut the thing in two at the waist. One of her trainees behind her finished it with the tip of his sword.

Since the first day, the queue to leave the gates had grown. Axle led her team of twelve out through the widening gap, every other protector with a similar party behind them. Only Magma—as the general overseer—didn't have a team to babysit.

A slow yawn from the gate's hinges, Spike watched the army leave, knowing he'd be in their number soon.

Finally their turn, Spike lifted his wheelbarrow, fighting against the tilt because of the overflowing bricks and rocks. When he felt confident he had it level, he leaned close to Hugh. "Every time I watch one of the protectors take down a diseased, it makes me want to be one even more."

"It makes me wish national service was over."

Spike smiled at his friend. "It'll be over soon enough."

"Hopefully it'll be over before I am."

Before Spike could say anything else, he heard sobbing beside him. Mercy De'ath from team Yeti. Pale skinned, almost white hair, and dressed in a white tracksuit. She looked like a ghost. Her eyes—bloodshot with grief—stood in stark contrast to the rest of her.

In an attempt at subtlety, Spike shifted closer and kept his focus on the exiting army. "Are you okay?"

Mercy fixed her red and swollen stare on Spike. The corners of her mouth dipped, and more tears ran down her cheeks.

"Are you scared?"

While pressing the back of her hand to her nose, she said, "What do you think?"

"Stupid question, right?"

She shrugged.

"Try not to be. Everything will be okay."

Mercy rolled her eyes.

"Okay, that wasn't helpful, but we've managed to take down over twenty diseased as a group."

"And lost an entire team on day one."

"But we're better at it already. What happened to Phoenix won't happen again." The protectors at the front of the group had reached the perimeter of the new wall and were venturing into the long grass, heading to the ruined city for another day of scavenging and killing. How many heads would they bring back with them? "The protectors will clear the way for us. There's over one hundred of them out there now. Everything will be fine."

The weight of Mercy's water bucket made her wobble as she picked it up. She nodded at him, her face locked in a grimace from the battle against the container of shifting liquid.

The last of the protectors entered the long grass. It wouldn't be long before Spike walked out there with them. What would he find in the city? What did the protectors know that they didn't tell Edin's citizens? How many secrets would he have to keep? Whatever orders they gave him, he'd tell Matilda everything. A glance at his love, he saw her fixed on the gates, her hair tied up, her soft eyes narrowed against the wind.

A gasp started with one or two cadets before the slightest rumblings ran through them all. Matilda turned to look behind them before Spike did. When he spun around, he saw Ranger striding towards them. His stomach lurched to look at the boy. The fight with Hugh had happened two days ago, and he hadn't seen him since. He looked like a different person. Where he'd had black bags beneath his eyes, they were now sacks. He looked like he hadn't slept since they took him away. He marched with his head dipped against the wind, his face slightly tilted towards the ground. He looked at the gates from beneath his thick brow, his jaw jutting out in a tight clench.

"What's *he* doing back?" Hugh said.

Bleach clapped his hands, and many of the cadets jumped. "Right, come on, let's get on with it. I want a productive day. We need to finish this wall sometime this decade."

Team Minotaur set off first, led by their team leader. Despite his curiosity telling him to look at Ranger—Hugh doing it several times—Spike couldn't take his eyes from his finely balanced barrow. Bleach might have allowed him to restrain Ranger in the canteen, but if he spilled a barrow of bricks from looking at the boy, he'd undo all the good favour he'd earned in a heartbeat. Nothing should get in the way of building the wall.

Outside the gates, the wind crashed into Spike, unsettling his fragile balance, his heart leaping as he fought to wrestle back control of the barrow. His attention ahead, he scanned the gaps in the wall. Ranger didn't matter when diseased could show up at any moment. Despite the army of protectors going out before them, they had to remain vigilant.

The teams fanned out behind Minotaur, and when they were far enough away, Hugh spoke to Bleach. "What happened to Ranger?"

"He spent thirty-six hours in the hole."

The words quickened Spike's pulse and he spoke before Hugh could. "*Thirty-six hours?* Do you think it's worked?"

"We offered for him to take today off and he declined. He said he's ready to face the diseased. I suppose only time will tell."

Max glanced over at Bigfoot. "If looks are anything to go by, he appears ready to fight."

Olga scoffed. "And as long as he survives, we all know Daddy will get him a free pass into the trials."

"If he lasts that long," Heidi said. "He looks like a liability at the moment. Hopefully he doesn't get anyone else killed if he goes down."

Spike kept his thoughts about the trials to himself. He didn't resent Max wanting to get into them, but it felt odd to talk openly about them in front of him.

CHAPTER 10

More cuts covered Spike's hands, his knuckles ached, and a deep twinge spasmed at the base of his back. He wiped his sweating brow and drew a lungful of the meadow-scented air. Max currently mixed the clay, grass, and water for him. Elizabeth dug the grave. Spike said, "If I never build another wall again, it will be too soon."

Before Max could reply, Bleach—who stood with Hugh, Heidi, and Olga on guard—perked up. "Problem, William?"

After drawing a sigh, Spike winced through another sharp muscle spasm and continued building the wall.

Bleach stepped towards Spike as if to press the issue, but as he opened his mouth, a scream burst from the long grass.

Dropping the brick in his hand, Spike stood up and unsheathed his sword in one fluid motion.

While scanning the meadow between them and the ruined city in the distance, Bleach said, "Calm down, everyone; we don't know who they're going to attack. We've decided to continue with the new strategy since Phoenix fell. There's nothing to worry about. Just follow my lead like we've done plenty of times already."

Bleach backed inside the perimeter of the broken wall.

Tightly gripping his sword, Spike followed his leader with the rest of his team. The second they were inside the wide and broken masonry arc, he glanced at Matilda. She looked ready. She'd cope just fine.

Like they'd done on their first day outside the walls, the teams formed a line. No one spoke.

Suddenly two diseased children burst through a gap on Spike's right. Two girls, they couldn't have been any older than eight. They paused, scanning the cadets and team leaders as if ascertaining who to attack. They looked like twins, but it could have been the effects of the virus that made them appear similar.

With his own pulse throbbing in his ears, Spike twisted his sore grip tighter. He spoke in a murmur. "Come on, then, you little bastards."

But they broke to the right instead. Screaming at a pitch higher than many of the others, they ran with their little hands thrust out in front of them. It was as if they smelled Mercy's fear.

When Spike stepped towards her, Bleach grabbed his shoulder and pulled him back. Turning on his team leader, Spike tried to shake himself free. "Let me go."

Bleach gripped Spike's shirt and pulled a sharp tug on it. "No! They have to look after themselves. You *know* that. Don't break ranks. You saw what happened to Phoenix."

Although Spike pulled against his team leader, he couldn't remove himself from his grasp. "But you saw her this morning. She's in no state to fight them."

"Let the girl fight and let her team protect her. You can't save everyone, William."

"No, but I can save *her*."

The debate had taken his advantage away. The children were now too close.

Although she'd watched them the entire way, Mercy still

hadn't lifted her sword. Her face buckled with her tears, and her arms hung limp by her sides.

Cupping his mouth, Spike screamed so loud it tore at his throat. "Fight them. Fight them off."

Mercy didn't react.

The first of the diseased girls leaped from the ground and flew towards Mercy, her mouth open wide. She hit her hard, knocking them both down. The child bit at her face.

Before the second of the two girls could go for anyone else in team Yeti, Ranger shrieked. A call similar to the sound the diseased made, it lifted the hairs on the back of Spike's neck and sent a cold chill through his body. The boy had lost his mind.

The diseased girl charged at him.

Spike watched the girl who'd bitten Mercy jump up and join her twin. Where he'd seen Ranger run away just a week ago, he now watched him yell and step forward to meet them. He swung his sword in a wide vertical arc that ended in the top of the first girl's head. As her legs buckled beneath her, he pulled his weapon from her skull before she fell. A wide swing decapitated the next one. He stamped on her pallid face, turning her off like her sister.

Mercy remained on her back, her face glistening with blood from the fresh wound. Ranger ran over to her, ignoring Juggernaut's calls to stop him intervening.

A second later, Mercy snarled and Ranger stamped down hard on her like he had with the little girl. The maniacal grimace locking his features looked somewhere between insanity and joy. Spike couldn't tell which. His teeth bared, his eyes wide, he stamped on Mercy again, his foot slipping from her bleeding face several times before her skull finally cracked.

But the boy kept going, every stomp pulping Mercy's head until Spike couldn't tell if the squelch came from her brain or the damp mud it had been mashed into.

Olga shook her head. "My god, he's lost it."

As they watched Ranger, many of the cadets around them sobbing from what they saw, Spike said, "Bleach, you have to do something."

But Bleach didn't move. Not his cadet to manage, he watched Juggernaut finally go over to Ranger, approaching with caution as he talked him down.

It took for Juggernaut to call the boy's name several times before he stopped and looked at his team leader, his teeth still bared from his frenzied attack. Spike saw the tears running down his cheeks.

Juggernaut kept his distance, allowing Ranger to step away from the downed Mercy. It looked like he'd forgotten about the other cadets, his expression softening when he took in his audience. Some of the cadets close to him moved back a step. A slow scan of those around him, he stopped when he made eye contact with Spike. If Spike thought he had an easy ride to becoming the next apprentice, he had another think coming.

Spike turned to Bleach. "Mercy didn't have to die then."

A slight narrowing of his green eyes, the sides of Bleach's jaw widened and relaxed as if clenching it helped him hold onto his retort.

CHAPTER 11

The rain came down so hard it stung. Spike squinted as he watched the guards on either side of the gates turn the wheels, the chains rushing over the wood at high speed.

Despite them being over three weeks into national service, Spike's pulse quickened as he waited to go outside. Fear and excitement in equal measure. If he survived, he'd be lining up in front of the gates in the near future. Better to be a protector than someone like Bleach: a glorified schoolteacher who put the rules first, even if it meant sacrificing those who didn't need to die. As a protector, he'd be able to make sure people like Mercy didn't perish unnecessarily.

Even with his sword strapped to his back, Spike could almost feel the handle in his grip as he waited for the diseased to burst through the gates. If they needed him, he'd join the fight. Not that Magma would want him there. The hero protector still fixed him with a death stare similar to many he'd received from his son.

It took for Hugh to say, "Huh?" for Spike to notice the confused looks on the protectors' faces. The team leaders mirrored their expressions, many of them shrugging at one another.

"No diseased?" Max said.

After watching the gates for a few more seconds, Spike turned to his teammates. "Has that ever happened before?"

None of them replied. And how would they know? They'd only been going outside for a few weeks too.

It took several seconds of the protectors looking at one another before Magma took the lead, walking out through the widening gap in the gates. He had Jezebel raised, but as he walked farther, he lowered her.

The gates opened wider and Spike saw the long grass beyond the wall. It bent and swayed, submissive to the weather. But there were no diseased outside.

Heidi finally answered him. "I'd guess from the looks on their faces, this is the first time it's happened."

Despite the clear confusion of the hundred or so protectors, none of them hesitated in following their leader, or looked back. They never looked back. Instead, they marched towards the long grass in the direction of the ruined city beyond.

"Maybe they're finally dying out?"

Olga snorted a derisive laugh at Hugh. "What are you on?"

A red flush lit Hugh's face and he dropped his focus to the ground. "I dunno. We can hope, can't we?"

"Hopes don't get you very far in this world," Olga said. "You should work harder on your wits and guile."

Where the teams would normally set off after the protectors, Bleach looked at the other leaders as if awaiting their approval. It came in the form of Juggernaut leading team Bigfoot out, Tank and team Dragon following behind. Bleach shrugged before leading his team out after them.

The heavy barrow pulled on the aches and pains in Spike's back, the soft ground sapping his strength as the wheel sank into it. It had been over a fortnight since Mercy's death. Not much had happened since. Diseased had appeared and been slain. Some more of the wall had been built. They all felt exhausted. But at least there hadn't been any more deaths. Other than when Mercy fell, their new plan to pull back and hold their line inside the wall had proven effective.

Easier to look at Ranger without the boy looking back, Spike watched him stride out just behind Juggernaut. If he'd said anything since his last trip to the hole, Spike hadn't witnessed it. The rumour in the camp was that he hadn't even spoken to Lance. From the way Lance walked—in the wake of his hero, but definitely separate from him—those rumours appeared to be true. Something had changed in him since that last trip. Where he'd been an arsehole before, he now took it to a whole new level. Sheer toxicity emanated from his stocky form. But he'd come back a better fighter. His fear of the diseased had been well and truly vanquished.

The barrow gave Spike more resistance with every step, the soggy ground eating away at his momentum. He clenched his jaw, fighting to maintain his forward progress while keeping the thing stable. If he stopped, he wouldn't get moving again. Sweating beneath his clothes, he kept a hard squint against the weather's brutal assault. At least it was May. Rain, he could cope with. Rain in freezing conditions … Thank god he had his birthday when he did. Screw doing this in the middle of winter.

Harder to see because of the harsh weather, Spike looked beyond the line of protectors at the ruined city. It represented freedom. When he visited it for the first time, he'd be a protector. He'd be able to save whoever needed saving. He'd be living in Edin with Matilda. He only needed to keep his head down and appease those above him for another four months. No way could they pick Ranger, even if they let him on the trials. No one would want to go outside the wall with that kind of liability.

The sound of rushing chains signalled the closing gates. The rookies continued moving towards their parts of the wall at a slow trudge.

Hugh then yelled, "Matilda!"

Spike's heart leapt. He dropped his barrow and drew his sword with a ring of steel.

The other cadets stopped too.

When Spike saw no immediate danger, he spoke from the side of his mouth. "You'd better have had a good reason to shout her name."

Clearly feeling the pressure of everyone watching, Hugh's voice warbled when he said, "Come with me."

Despite the scrutiny of the cadets and team leaders alike, Spike followed Hugh through the still-stationary teams in Matilda's direction.

As they got closer, Matilda grew redder. "What are you two doing?"

Hugh reached around and pulled Matilda's sword free. Had many other people done it, Matilda would have resisted, but she trusted Hugh because Spike trusted him, although he was certainly testing her confidence in him right now.

"Hugh!" Bleach said. "What the *hell* are you doing?"

Again, Hugh didn't reply. Instead, he lifted Matilda's sword while drawing his own with his other hand. He banged the two together. Matilda's sword broke at the hilt and split into three separate pieces.

As Matilda gasped, Spike looked at the shocked faces of those around him. Everyone looked their way, everyone but Ranger, who continued to watch the protectors wading through the long grass as if the drama meant nothing to him.

Tank—team Dragon's leader—shook his head while looking at the now closed gates. "It's too late to go back. I'll keep you on the wall today. We'll have to protect you."

When Spike drew his sword, Tank's eyes narrowed. Spike held it, handle first, in Matilda's direction. "Take mine."

She shook her head.

"*Please* take mine."

The cadets and team leaders all watched on before Ranger shouted, "Just take it, Matilda. We have a wall to build. None of us care about your lovers' tiff."

But Matilda refused Spike's offer again. Before he could argue, Hugh did the same with his weapon. "Please take mine. I agree with you about Spike needing his, but I don't even know how to use this thing. We stand a much better chance as a group with you and Spike armed than we do with me and Spike armed.

A slight weakening in her resolve, Matilda took Hugh's sword and dipped him a subtle bow. "Thank you."

Hugh nodded before returning to the bucket of water he'd set down with his team. Spike and Matilda shared a lingering look before Spike ran after the boy.

When they were back at their tools, the rest of the cadets having already moved off, Spike said, "Thank you. She needed that."

Hugh shrugged. "Like I said, she can do much more with it than I can."

CHAPTER 12

His barrow now filled with rocks and bricks, Spike watched Hugh lift a bucket of water. They'd returned to the gates to restock their supplies. So soaked, his sodden clothes restricted his movement. The rain still hadn't let up. "There's something not right about today."

"There's something not right about most days. It's called a shit ton of diseased ready to descend on us at any moment. I've started having nightmares about them."

"Be honest, you've always had nightmares about them."

Although Hugh opened his mouth to reply, no words came out.

"Anyway, it's something else."

"Something more than our imminent death?"

"Our imminent death I can deal with; that's normal for national service. But why were there no diseased this morning?"

"You're complaining about there being no diseased? *Surely* that's a good thing?"

"You saw how they reacted. There's something strange about it. Also, why was Matilda's sword broken?"

"They're not the best weapons. The only reason ours don't fall apart is because I service them."

"How did you know hers was broken?"

"The main screw was missing. There was a shiny silver circle where it should be. It stands out when you know the swords as intimately as I do."

"Missing or taken?"

Hugh shrugged.

"It just doesn't seem right."

"But what can we do about it other than keep our heads down, work on the wall, and remain alert? We have to keep calm and carry on. It's not like the leaders will give us time off because we're a bit freaked out. We're supposed to be freaked out; it's national service."

Mercy's death came back to Spike as he looked at the cadets working on the wall. They were all busy on their own sections, the rain coming down so hard it bounced. "I don't like—"

The scream of a diseased pierced the air. It cut through the lashing rain and strong wind. Hard to tell where it came from, Spike looked in what he assumed to be its direction. Somewhere near Dragon and Bigfoot. Between Ranger and Matilda. He lowered his barrow and drew his sword.

Nearly one thousand feet between where they stood and the two teams. Spike bounced on the balls of his feet, ready to take off. If he went now, he might get there in time.

Another scream.

"It sounds like it's going to hit Dragon?"

Although Spike asked it as a question, looking for the excuse to charge into battle, Hugh didn't reply.

He had to make a choice.

The screams of more diseased joined the first.

Then Spike saw them. Three creatures, they burst through the hole in the wall closest to Dragon. They ran straight at Matilda.

The desire to run surging through him, Spike's chest tightened. His attention on Matilda, he said, "I won't make it. They don't even have the time for everyone to fall back."

If he ran over to help, he'd face the wrath of both Bleach and Matilda. And for what? To get there when the fight had finished.

Matilda drew her sword, the muscles in Spike's upper body twitching as if he did every move with her. She swung for the first of the pallid and uncoordinated beasts, her sword landing in its neck.

The creature went down as she turned on the next one, driving the blade of her weapon into the centre of its face.

It also fell.

A scream louder than any made by the diseased, Matilda yelled while raising her sword to attack the third, but she didn't move quickly enough. The beast took her down and landed on top of her.

Spike's breathing quickened and his stomach clamped tight. The first creature she'd hit then jumped up, its head flopping to the side from where it had only been partly severed from its body.

Ginger Slink moved fast, finishing the job Matilda had started by taking its head clean off. Tank stamped down, crushing it. He then kicked the diseased off Matilda, Nancy Humberto lunging forward and stabbing its head. But Matilda remained on the ground.

Another scream, another diseased. This time it went for Bigfoot. Ranger had the strength and rage to decapitate it with one swing.

It started as a twitching leg before Matilda jumped to her feet. Those around her drew their swords. It took all Spike had to remain standing. He should have run to her.

CHAPTER 13

The fierce rain and tears in his eyes made it impossible for Spike to watch it play out. Probably for the best. He'd just lost everything that mattered. But then Hugh tugged on his sleeve. "She's okay."

Spike gasped as Matilda raised her hands in the air, those around her not fully lowering their weapons, but giving her the chance to plead her case. Tank instructed her to take her top off, so she stood in front of them in just a bra. Fury boiled in Spike's stomach, but Tank had to inspect her for bites and cuts.

As much as he didn't want to look, Spike saw Ranger watching her. The same hatred burned in his dark features, but the violence he stared at her had a tinge of lust. Hopefully the diseased would take him down soon.

Loud enough for them all to hear, Tank yelled, "She's okay. She's not been bitten."

As much as Spike wanted to cheer, he kept it to himself. Many had died and many more would die. They shouldn't celebrate the life of one over others. For a moment, he made eye contact with Matilda and dipped a nod at her, tears now running down his cheeks. Maybe she nodded back, he couldn't tell.

Spike then grabbed Hugh and pulled him in for a tight hug, his tears gushing out of him. "Thank you," he said. "Without your sword, she would have died. Thank you so much."

While patting Spike's back, Hugh laughed. "Anytime, buddy. Anytime."

CHAPTER 14

Had Spike been on the gates yesterday with what felt like a straight day of rain and having nearly lost Matilda, the miserable job would have been even more miserable. They'd gotten to the end of their first month, and team Dragon had been awarded the extra day off. If they'd based it purely on the amount of diseased slain, Bigfoot would have gotten it, but Ranger trying to kill Hugh worked against them.

Because nothing ever happened on guard duty, they only needed one cadet to watch the gates. They took their sword away and swapped it for a horn. If—on the rare occasion—they needed help, all the cadet had to do was blow it and wait.

The sound of several diseased's screams snapped Spike from his thoughts, his heart racing. He listened to them on the other side of the gates, their awkward and uneven steps squelching in the wet ground. No doubt they were waiting until they opened in the morning.

Spike pressed his ear to the wooden barrier between them, the wind swaying the large gates and him by extension. It sounded like three or four of the vile things. Although he couldn't see them, he might gain valuable insight from the sounds they made.

Then he heard something else. The steps of another, except they sounded different. This one moved more easily. It moved fast and with even steps. A muted thud. Then another, another, and one more. The steps vanished into the distance.

Other than the strong wind, it left silence outside. What the hell did he just hear?

Spike stepped away from the gate and shook his head. Without seeing what had happened, he couldn't form any conclusions. Maybe he'd heard animals on the other side and his overactive imagination told him to expect more. Diseased didn't kill other diseased. He might have had the day off, but with it being so late, his mind had obviously started to play tricks on him.

Not the worst shift, Spike had pulled midnight until two a.m. Next time he would have two a.m. until four a.m., then four till five thirty, followed by five thirty till seven, and then back to ten till twelve. The ones at the start of the evening were longer because you could still get a good night's sleep when the shift wrapped up. Everyone hated four till five thirty—up super early and then back to the dorm to doze at best. It robbed them of their most valuable sleep.

Spike paced, walking up and down across the front of the gates. He looked at the tall wooden barriers and the wheels the guards turned. In his mind, he heard the chains running over the wood, the twenty-foot gates shaking before they parted, and he led a team of protectors out towards the ruined city. Soon he'd be the one clearing the way for the anxious rookies behind him. As much as he thought he'd wanted to be like Magma, now he'd seen him in action, he knew he'd enjoy it more than the surly man did. Sure, Magma fought like a hero, but Warrior ... now Warrior fought like he'd been born to do it.

Although the rain had eased, the poor weather brought a cold snap with it. Spike hugged himself for warmth and quickened his pace, the ground squelching beneath his steps. A tight clench to his jaw sent pains streaking up either side of his face, but it helped counter the teeth-rattling shiver that threatened to take over.

While walking the twenty or so feet before turning and going back the other way, Spike counted. Two hours with not much to do felt like a lifetime. He lengthened his strides and crossed the gap with just eighteen steps. The least he'd managed to do it in. "Yes," he said to himself, doing an impromptu jig before he spun around to walk the other way. But just as he set off again, he stopped. A silhouette stood in the darkness. It stared straight at him.

CHAPTER 15

Too dark to see who watched him, Spike held his distance. The figure didn't move either.

The tall gates threw the sound of his own voice back at him and highlighted the lifting pitch in his wavering words. "It's not two already, is it?"

The silhouette remained static.

On instinct, Spike reached for the sword on his back. Except he had no sword. Of course he didn't; they had to return their swords to their dorms at the end of every day. They weren't to be carried in the national service area. Instead, he pulled on the horn around his neck. Not exactly a deadly weapon, but he might need to sound an alarm before using the narrow end to stick his attacker.

Before he'd thought it through, Spike stamped his foot in the mud. "Who goes there?" The silence seemed more complete than ever, and he winced at his own demand. It sounded cool in the swashbuckling stories the teachers told them at school, but it had no place in the real world. Next he'd be telling the sucker to freeze or reach for the sky.

The silhouette moved and Spike stepped back, his hands

balled into fists. He went for his horn, but the silhouette moved forward again, the moonlight catching the silver clip in her hair. The next step revealed her face. "Tilly?"

She snorted a laugh. "*Who goes there?*"

The same tight clench to his jaw that kept his shivering at bay, Spike bit down as if it would help him hold onto his defensive response. It delayed it by milliseconds at best. "It sounded like the right thing to say."

"Good job slaying the diseased doesn't rely on you sounding cool, eh? You'd be shit out of luck."

"All right, smart-ass."

The gap between them now just a few feet, Spike lowered his voice. "What are you doing here? It's late."

"We have tomorrow off."

"Yeah, well done on that. You deserve it."

"As much as it pains me to say, Ranger deserved it the most, but he's a liability."

"Screw Ranger; he doesn't deserve anything. Not with how he went for Hugh. I'm just grateful the dullard dropped the knife." Spike continued to close the gap between him and Matilda until they were close enough for him to reach out and hold her hands. "I'm serious about you not sneaking up on me though."

A wry smile, Matilda lifted her eyebrows. "What? You might attack me?"

"Something like that."

"I'd kick your arse."

The reaction rose and died in Spike. After a deep breath, he shrugged. "I'm so glad Hugh saw your sword was broken before you were attacked. Imagine—"

"I'd rather not."

"Do you think someone did it on purpose?"

"I'm not sure thinking that way will get me anywhere. Unless

I *know* someone did it for sure, I think it's easier to assume it was an accident. They don't exactly give us the best quality weapons."

"You think they'd make more of an effort with them. It's hard enough fighting outside those walls." Just talking about it quickened his pulse. "If we do find out someone did it on purpose, I'll kill 'em."

It took for Matilda to let go of Spike's hands for him to realise he'd gripped them too tightly.

"I'm sorry. I get a bit emotional thinking about it."

"Just try to keep your head, okay?" This time Matilda grabbed Spike's hands and rubbed her thumbs over the backs of them. While tracing a heart, she said, "Thank you for your concern, and thank you for holding your ground when the diseased attacked me."

Although Spike opened his mouth to reply, she cut him off. "I know how hard it was for you to stand back and let me fight." She moved towards him. "For you to respect my wishes to make sure you don't kill yourself trying to save me. Artan needs one of us, so thank you. If we can both keep our heads, we'll have the future we've planned together."

Had Spike been closer to her yesterday, he would have been at her side in a heartbeat, but she didn't need to know that. Instead, he nodded, closing the much smaller gap between them, their lips touching.

When they pulled away, Spike stared into Matilda's deep brown eyes. They were glazed with the start of tears. "Are you okay?"

Matilda shrugged. "I just want this over with. I miss Artan and want to see how he's doing. I hate the work outside the walls. I'll have hands like a rock troll for months after we've finished national service. Ranger's also doing my head in. I could deal with him when he made a few basic misogynist comments to wind you up, but now he's gone psycho. I don't even want to be in the same area as him. He's so volatile."

Spike shuddered to think about the boy and how his second trip to the hole had changed him. The way he looked at everyone now like they were his enemy. The way he had looked at Matilda when she took her top off. Not that he'd share that with her. She'd be better off not knowing. But if he went anywhere near her, Spike would tie him to his bed and gouge his piggy little eyes out. "My hope is he gets himself either killed or kicked off national service."

"Can you imagine having to spend five months living with him in the training area?"

The thought unsettled the rhythm of Spike's breaths. "I don't want to think about it."

"I don't blame you."

"They did their first task yesterday."

"In the trials?"

"Yep."

Matilda looked in the direction of the wall separating them from the area they held the trials in. "We'll get through this, you know? And you'll smash it when you get there."

"I love you, Tilly."

Matilda leaned forward, kissed, and then hugged Spike again. They held on for a few seconds.

When they separated, Matilda said, "I need to get back now. I hope the rest of your shift goes okay and you get some good sleep for tomorrow."

"I'll be thinking of you when I'm out building a wall and you're in bed all day." He winked at her. "Next time they inspect you for bites, I might see if they need a volunteer."

Even in the moonlight, Spike saw Matilda's reddening cheeks. "When this is all over, you can check me for bites as much as you like."

Spike watched her vanish into the darkness, her sweet taste still on his lips. He filled his lungs and let the air out in a cloud of condensation before setting off and walking back across the front of the gate, counting his steps as he went.

~

Maybe ten minutes passed, maybe more, but when Spike saw another silhouette where Matilda had been, he smiled. "Come back to let me check for bites, then?"

Like the first time she'd arrived, Matilda didn't reply. Like the first time she'd arrived, she stepped forward. Like the first time she'd arrived, Spike tensed in anticipation of a fight. Then he laughed. "Come on, Tilly, stop being a goon."

When the silhouette stepped close enough for the moonlight to reveal them, Spike's stomach lurched. "What are *you* doing here?"

CHAPTER 16

Instead of replying, Ranger walked closer to Spike, the dark eyes Spike had fantasised about gouging from his fat head fixed on him.

Armed only with a horn, Spike froze and waited for the wide boy to get closer.

Just a few feet separated them before Spike raised a halting hand. "Stay back."

"Or what?"

Spike lifted the horn to his lips.

"You're going to tell on me?"

"You could do with another stint in the hole."

Ranger darted forward, the moonlight catching the knife in his hand just moments before Spike felt it at his throat, forcing him up against the gates.

The whites of Ranger's eyes ringed his dark irises, and he leaned so close Spike could smell his rancid breath. A spread of bared teeth, he spoke through his clenched jaw. "You're no stronger than me; you just got lucky. Go in the hole for a second time and you'll see. You swan around here acting like you're the shit, but you ain't. I'm going to prove that to you."

"By stabbing me? You're a *coward*."

Ranger smiled. His eyes didn't. "I'm not the one crying."

"You're a coward using a knife. And I'm not crying."

"Your eyes are watering." Ranger put more pressure on the weapon and Spike gulped against the sting of the tip. "This is to get you to listen. I *hate* you, Spike. I hate everything about you. I hate how you think you have a chance to become the next protector. I hate how you flaunt your relationship with Matilda. I hate how pally you are with that little mole you hang around with. Natural selection should have taken him out a long time ago."

The gate swayed with the wind. "Is that all you've come to say? I can already see the hatred in your beady little eyes; there's no need to articulate it."

Ranger reached into his pocket and produced a small steel bolt. "Recognise this?"

A torrent ran through Spike, but he fought against it. "Natural selection, eh?"

"What are you talking about?"

"Sometimes it takes more than brawn to survive. Hugh might not be the most physical of all the cadets, but he's one of the smartest. One of the most observant. Let's say you did jeopardise Matilda's weapon, which I'm not sure I believe anyway, Hugh was the one who noticed. He was the one who scuppered your plan. *Another* failure on your part."

"Another one?"

"You want me to list them? On day one you ran away."

Ranger put more pressure on the knife.

"Then you tried to attack Hugh, but your clumsy hands dropped the weapon before you reached him."

"You think I have difficulties holding a knife?"

Spike stood on his tiptoes to relieve the pressure of the blade. "Let's say I believe you messed with Matilda's sword; what have you shown me so far to prove you're a threat?"

"I have a knife to your throat right now, Spike."

"Which you just said you won't use. I believe that. I don't think you have the minerals, and we both know you won't get away with it if you do."

Ranger's breathing sped up and he moved his face even closer to Spike's. He pushed the knife and Spike felt a warm trickle of blood run down the inside of his shirt. "Just know I'm going to make your life hell. You're like a spider that I'm going to pull the legs off one at a time. Hugh, Matilda, Olga, Elizabeth … You're going to try to save them, because that's what you do, right? But you can't save all of them. And every time you try, you jeopardise your chances of going on the trials. You're going to wish you never crossed me."

"I *didn't* cross you. You're the one who's clearly threatened by me."

Another tight clench to his jaw, Ranger spat on the gate next to Spike's face before he pulled back. A slight smile lifted his wicked sneer. "I enjoyed watching Matilda being checked for bite marks."

A chill snapped through Spike. "How long have you been in the shadows for?"

"Let's hope they have to do it again." He flicked the small metal bolt. It hit Spike just below his left eye, a sharp sting making his vision blur.

While letting go of a long exhale, Spike watched Ranger walk away. He wiped his watering eyes and bleeding neck. As much as he didn't want to believe what Ranger had just said, he believed every word. They had four months ahead of them, and not only did he have to make sure he did everything required of him to be selected for the trials, but he now needed to make sure Ranger didn't get his friends and loved ones killed in the process.

CHAPTER 17

At least Spike could go outside the walls without having to worry about Matilda's safety. Although, after his run-in with Ranger the previous evening, he clearly had to worry about the safety of many of those around him.

Hugh stretched his arms to the sky, releasing a groaning yawn. His brown eyes were glazed and his cheeks red. "That early shift's a killer."

Even though Spike heard him, he watched Ranger, looking for some sign as to what he planned next. "I'm glad Tilly's safe inside the gates today."

"What about us? We could do with a day off."

Spike continued to watch Ranger. "We'll cope."

"Are you okay?"

If Spike told Hugh about the previous evening, it would only make him worry. "I'm fine. Sorry. Don't fret about today. We'll be all right."

The reassurance clearly did little for Hugh, who unsheathed his sword and inspected it. Once he'd done with his, he held his hand out to take a look at Elizabeth's weapon, then Spike's,

Olga's, Max's, and Heidi's. "Well, at least our swords won't fall apart on us."

Spike rubbed the spot beneath his left eye where Ranger had hit him with the bolt.

At that moment, the protectors appeared, making their way through the crowd as they headed for the gates. Magma, who normally led the line, took up the rear, making a point to look at Spike with the same callous regard he'd grown used to from his progeny. Did he know anything about the night before? Had he encouraged his boy to do it?

"What happened to your neck?" Hugh said.

Like with his cheek, Spike reached up and touched where Ranger had hurt him the previous evening. Although he could feel the nasty boy watching him, he kept his focus on his old man, who joined the other protectors in front of the gates. "I cut it shaving."

As with Ranger, Spike felt Hugh looking at him as if he wanted a better explanation.

Magma nodded at the guards on the gate, the air coming alive with the barrelling sound of the heavy chains. It dragged Hugh's attention from Spike.

All seven protectors stood ready, their teams lined up behind them. They all had their weapons raised, their stances solid as they waited for the morning rush. But the only sound came from the chains running over wood, the gates swaying as they slowly moved inwards. First a split, the gap then grew wider.

The noises from the previous evening returned to Spike. He'd definitely heard diseased out there. Not so unusual, but the steps of something much more coordinated than the diseased certainly were. The thuds and then nothing. What could have made those sounds?

The gap had grown wide enough for an atrophied limb to

reach through, but none did. The protectors looked at one another. No diseased for a second time?

Olga said, "What the hell? There's normally a ton of them on a Monday. I think they're finally dying out."

A hard scowl hooded Bleach's green eyes. "You think like that and you'll be the one dying out."

"So what's happening?"

"I wish I knew."

The gap in the gates now wide enough for the protectors to exit, Fire led the line, taking his team with him. The remaining protectors followed, one team at a time. They all kept their weapons raised. They all searched from left to right as if they were walking into an ambush.

When the protectors had passed through, Bleach motioned for them to move. Spike lifted the heavy barrow's handles and followed his team towards their section of the wall.

∽

Paranoia isn't always a bad thing. Paranoia kept many a rookie alive outside the walls. As Spike studied the long grass between him and the ruined city, Olga on one side, Heidi on the other, he said, "I feel like I'm being watched."

Olga laughed while Heidi's already tense frame tightened.

When she'd finished laughing, Olga said, "Watching is the last thing those things will be doing. If they've seen you, you can bet your arse they're running at you. They don't have it in them to *watch*."

Were he talking to Hugh or Matilda, Spike might have taken the conversation further. Instead, he looked at the ruined city and filled his lungs with the fresh meadow's scent. Breathing felt easier out here despite the threats to their lives. The air had a palpable humidity that made it cool and soothing. But today there seemed to be a tinge on the breeze. Maybe paranoia had the same vinegar reek as the diseased. He watched the swaying grass and twisted his feet to strengthen his stance.

Olga had clearly been waiting for a reply. When it didn't come, she said, "No, the diseased don't watch, they—"

The shrieks of several diseased rang out.

"—scream and charge," Olga said while drawing her broadsword. "Here we go again."

They'd done it enough times to know the drill, but Bleach gave the orders anyway. "Fall back inside the walls and form a line. Let them come to you."

Spike fell back with the rest of the cadets.

Enough wall around them to make Bleach's words echo. "Hold the line."

Too far away from team Cyclops to do anything about it, Spike—who stood next to Bleach—watched five diseased burst through a gap in the wall and charge them.

Farther forward than the rest of her team by a few feet, the diseased clearly sensed the weakness and zeroed in on Dionne White. While Cyclops moved back a few paces, she froze, singled out more than before.

"She should be moving back with them," Bleach said.

Like when he'd watched Matilda from the gates, Spike felt powerless to do anything. "Why don't they help her?"

"They're trying to."

"By stepping away?"

"By moving back and regrouping. They're trying to get into a stronger position to fight."

Ore's words cracked through the mostly enclosed space. "Dionne! Fall back!"

If Dionne heard her, she didn't react.

There were rumours amongst the cadets about certain couples hooking up. Spike and Matilda, Hugh and Elizabeth, Dionne

White and Juan Costa from team Yeti. Where Dionne's team weren't helping, Juan broke ranks and ran to her aid. Flame—his team leader—called after him. It did nothing to slow him down.

To hear Bleach mutter, "Stupid boy," lifted bile in Spike's throat, and he said, "He's just looking after a friend."

"Heroes and fools die on this side of the gates. It's hard to tell the difference between them sometimes, and the diseased don't discriminate."

"He's a hero."

"From the mouth of a fool."

Spike clenched his jaw to help him contain his words.

Juan drew his sword and drove it through the chest of the first diseased. When the creature fell, Spike smiled to see him finish it by stabbing the thing in the face. While yelling a battle cry, he hacked an arm from the next one before splitting the head of the third and then fourth.

"He's good," Spike said.

"He's a fool. Cutting an arm off a diseased doesn't …" Bleach left his words hanging, the armless diseased leaping at Dionne. It bit into her shoulder. Team Cyclops closed in on her at Ore's command.

The team leader dispatched the one-armed creature while Juan killed the fifth one.

Then Ore stood back, and although Spike couldn't hear what she said to Juan, he didn't need to. She pointed at the fallen Dionne, who held the top of her arm and screamed. Blood seeped through the gaps in her fingers.

Once again team Cyclops backed away at Ore's order.

Spike shook his head. "Why isn't *she* going to kill her?"

"Juan's the hero," Bleach said. "Now he needs to do the dirty work. That's what a hero is in this life."

Nauseated by the thought of having to end Matilda, Spike's throat dried.

Juan cried freely, his shoulders shaking while he raised his broadsword, tip down as he hung it over his girlfriend's face.

As Dionne fell silent, Spike held his breath. The wind and Juan's sobs were the only sounds out there, the gathered rookies all watching the boy.

Maybe she felt sorry for him because Ore stepped forward and said, "Do you need me to—?"

Dionne's diseased shriek cut her off.

A hero when fighting diseased he didn't know, but when Dionne jumped to her feet, Juan froze like she had. The former team Cyclops member—dressed in her blue tracksuit—continued forward in one fluid movement, latching onto Juan's throat as she took them both down.

They'd already hit the ground when Ore caught up to them. She stabbed Dionne through the back of her head and Juan through his face, cutting off his diseased shriek from where he'd turned almost instantly.

The wind filled the silence before Bleach released a long sigh. "That's what happens to fools out here. Heroes don't fare much better. You'd do well to learn from that."

The teams around the dead bodies moved back to their parts of the wall, dragging the corpses with them. Spike watched on without moving, the rest of Minotaur heading back to where they were working.

Hugh waited with him. "I can't believe Ore didn't help him with Dionne."

"I think she was right. Juan wanted to be a hero. He needed to do it."

"Would you do it for Tilly?"

Spike watched his team move around the other side of the wall out of sight. Most of the teams were back at the parts they were working on. Only a couple of team Cyclops remained: Tom French and Shannon Flung. They looked like they needed a moment, a diseased at their feet, which they'd clearly been tasked with removing.

When Spike saw the diseased twitch, he gasped.

Hugh cupped his mouth, calling across the space at Tom and Shannon, "It's not dead! It's not dead!"

CHAPTER 18

Tom and Shannon jumped away from the creature as it leaped to its feet. It hit Shannon first, Tom shrieking as he tripped and fell backwards. Before he'd hit the ground, it had bitten Shannon and crashed on top of him.

Spike's jaw hung open at the speed of the thing. Tom was already infected when it stood up again and scanned its surroundings as if looking for its next target.

Many of the cadets were by their walls, but Ranger headed back inside the perimeter. He stood between Spike and Hugh, and the vile creature. One, and then three diseased ran at him. Sword raised, he looked ready to take the one at the front down. But when it got close and lunged for him, he dodged it, the beast thundering past. And maybe it would have turned back around were Spike and Hugh not next in line.

Instead of waiting for the beast to get to them, Hugh shrieked and ran for the gates. "Someone sound the horn! Someone sound the horn!"

Spike yelled too, trying to get the attention of the diseased. "Come and get me, you freaks."

But like frenzied bulls, all three creatures zeroed in on the moving target.

Although he only had a second to think, Spike saw Ranger smiling at him. He'd done it on purpose. Of course he had.

Despite Bleach calling, "Don't follow him," Spike set off after his small friend. Not the fastest, Hugh stood no chance of getting to the gates before the diseased reached him. And no way would the guards open them for him if he had three of them on his tail.

His sword heavy on his back, Spike chased after Hugh while Bleach's voice chased after him. "I said don't follow him."

The thunder of uneven steps ran after Hugh. The screams from their foetid mouths echoed around him. Spike gritted his teeth and dug deep, quickening his pace, drawing on everything he had.

But he didn't have enough. The strength damn near left his legs to watch the first diseased jump onto Hugh's back, taking both of them to the ground.

CHAPTER 19

Although his body threatened to, Spike didn't give up. Just feet between him and the diseased on top of Hugh, he drew his sword and beat Tom and Shannon to his friend.

The beast on Hugh's back reared up, its mouth opened wide.

Spike kicked it before it could take a bite, sending the thing sprawling.

Shannon came at Spike next. He hacked at the side of her head and split her skull, wincing away from the spray of warm blood.

Tom rushed in a second later. Spike drove the tip of his sword into the front of his face, turning the boy off, but Tom's momentum ripped the sword from his hands, taking it with him as he fell dead on the ground.

The shrill scream of the first diseased exploded through the air; it then ran at Spike.

Only a second to react, Spike heard Hugh call his name. He turned to see the boy's sword coming at him. Despite the diseased's thunderous approach, he focused on the airborne weapon, caught it by the handle, and continued its momentum in a swing aimed at the beast's neck.

Enough to wound the creature and knock it to the ground. Spike stood over it and used both hands to drive the tip of Hugh's sword into its face, burying it into the soft ground beneath.

Sweat ran into Spike's eyes and he fought for breath while staring down at the pinned creature. When Hugh crashed into his side, he just managed to remain standing, accepting the hug from his friend, but not returning it.

Spike finally looked up to see the cadets had pulled back inside the perimeter of the wall. All of them watched him. He looked at Ranger and the bitter twist on his face. He wouldn't let him win. He'd save his friends no matter how many times the little psychopath tried to kill them. Then he turned his attention to Bleach. Too much distance between them for his team leader to say anything, he looked like he wanted to tear him a new one. But it didn't matter what Bleach said, Spike wouldn't ever let his friends die.

CHAPTER 20

As Spike watched the last person leave the canteen, he shoved his dirty dinner plate aside and rested his elbows on the table in front of him. A lot had happened in the last twenty-four hours. A late night on guard duty where Ranger had turned up, put a knife to his throat, and told him about Matilda's sword. Although, he still hadn't decided whether he spoke the truth. The boy would do anything to get under his skin. Then he'd had to go against Bleach's orders to save Hugh, which again Ranger had played a hand in. More cadets had died, and now as punishment—as if the last day hadn't been bad enough—he had to clean the dining hall.

The doors to the dining hall opened, and Spike turned around to see Bleach. "I'm getting on with it, okay? It's been a long day. I just need a moment before I start."

A few seconds of silence followed, the wind from outside entering the hall through the open door. The slightest smirk lifted one side of Bleach's mouth.

"You think this is funny?"

Bleach cut in. "Careful, William. I'm not here to berate you, so don't make me change my mind."

"Then why *are* you here? You've told me to clean the dining hall, which I intend to do."

"I'm not allowed to praise you for today."

"But?"

"Hugh's an important member of the team. I'm glad he's not dead. And you have the potential to be a great protector. Try not to jeopardise that. I'd like to go on my break after this national service knowing you've given yourself every chance to be selected."

Although Spike opened his mouth, Bleach turned away and walked off into the early evening, letting the dining hall door close behind him.

It gave Spike the jump-start he needed. Starting with his table, he grabbed the plates around him and stacked them one on top of the other.

∽

Nearly all the plates cleared away, Spike got to where Ranger sat. The dishes he and Lance had used were on the table and free of food—as were most of the plates; the cadets worked too hard to skip meals. But in the centre of both of them swam enough saliva and mucus to cover the bottom of each one. To look at it clamped tension through Spike's stomach, and he tasted bile in the back of his throat.

After a second, he lifted the plates. His shoulders were so taut it felt like they might not uncoil again. But what could he do? Of all the battles he had ahead of him, this seemed like one he should let go. He'd make Ranger pay in other ways. He just needed to make sure he was smart about it. Bide his time. If he reacted to provocation, he'd come unstuck.

∽

After he'd stacked the dirty dishes in the kitchen, Spike wiped the tables and was currently mopping the floor. He looked out through the large windows at the gates. The cadets and leaders had all returned to their dorms. The setting sun highlighted everything with a burned orange tinge, and the air had turned grainy as day transitioned to night.

Spike looked at the two guards on the gate. At least he'd done his night shift for the next few days. But it would come around again soon—sooner than he would have liked; fewer cadets meant more guard duty. They'd also have to build the wall quicker, carry more supplies, and be better fighters. How many would be left at the end of the five months?

It didn't help that Spike had to clean the dining hall on top of everything else. But if it meant he still had a chance for the apprenticeship trials, he'd clean the dining hall every evening. Not that he'd tell Bleach that. Less than four months until the trials and less than ten months before he'd be able to start living the life he wanted. It would all be worth it. Of course, from the looks Matilda had given him when they were having dinner, she was furious, but she'd come around. Especially when everything worked out.

The room now smelled of lavender like Bleach's dorm. Spike put the mop in the bucket and headed for the kitchen to attack the mountain of dirty dishes. However, before he could get there, the door hinges released a sinister groan. It stopped him in his tracks.

CHAPTER 21

"*Elizabeth?*" The perfect partner for Hugh. As much mouse as he was mole, she had long brown hair, sticking-out ears, and her front teeth were slightly oversized. "Are you okay? Is Hugh all right?"

She let the door close behind her before smiling and dipping the slightest nod. "We're both fine."

"Then …"

"What can you help me with? I was hoping I could help you. I've been waiting for Bleach to leave the dorm so I can come over and lend a hand. I wanted to say thanks for saving Hugh's life today."

Spike carried the bucket and mop towards the kitchen, peering at the stack of dirty dishes. He'd already filled the sink with cold water. When he saw Elizabeth follow him, he waited for her to catch up before walking through the door. "You two have gotten quite close, huh?"

"Yeah. He's a sweetie. He's kind to me."

"It goes a long way." After setting the bucket down, Spike plunged a plate into the cold water, grabbed a cloth, and cleaned it. When he put it down on the side, Elizabeth picked it up and dried it with a towel before putting it on a rack, ready to be used for breakfast.

It seemed like too obvious a question, but Spike needed to know. "So what are your plans after we're done here?"

"When Hugh and I go back to separate districts?"

The slightest numbness already spread through Spike's knuckles from the frigid water. Thank god he didn't have to do this in the height of winter; it would turn his hands into claws. "It's an obvious question. You don't seem like the kind of person to go into politics."

"What's that supposed to mean?"

"You have a shred of humanity."

"Thanks. I think. And I don't want to be a protector either."

"Well, that leaves f—"

"Hugh thinks we can both work in the labs and live on the campus there."

"And your family?"

"I'll miss them."

"But …?"

The slightest twist turned her soft features momentarily jagged. "Life isn't what you think it is in the woodwork district."

Spike handed her another clean plate before tipping a tray of cutlery into the sink, the rush of metal hitting the bottom.

"They have gangs there."

"*Gangs?*"

"Youths on the street who are controlled by some right horrible bastards higher up. It's insane. Between the ages of eighteen and twenty-two, life's hell if you belong to a gang, but it's worse if you don't. They tend to leave you alone after that."

"But four years is a long time."

"Right."

"And the guards don't do anything about it?"

"The guards are afraid of them. The gangs have such a tight

grip on the woodwork district, and there's so many of them, if they chose to revolt, Edin would fall. The last guard that stuck his nose in ended up dying in a warehouse fire. His entire family was in there with him too. Twelve of them in total from eight months to eighty. Every one of them died with the promise cousins would be involved next time."

"I heard about that fire."

"Didn't hear about why it happened though, did you?"

"No."

"Instead, it would have been told as a tragic accident to befall a poor innocent man and his *entire* family. Because a guard and his family would be spending the night in a warehouse ..."

"So what's the point of the gangs?"

"They want to live a life of freedom."

"Don't we all."

"They give the government enough output from the workshops to keep them off their backs. They then manage the distribution of rations."

"Giving themselves the largest slice of the pie."

"Of course." After drawing a deep breath, Elizabeth put the next plate down, tucked her long brown hair behind her ears, and lifted her top.

Spike turned away, raising a hand so he didn't have to look at her exposed body. "What are you doing?"

But she stopped lifting when she revealed the scar on her stomach. A five-pointed star, the angry red wound looked fresh. "They tag you before you go on national service. A reminder of who you belong to." After a pause, her eyes swelling with tears, she spoke with shaking words. "When you belong to a gang, they do what they want with you."

It turned Spike's stomach to think about it. "As in ...?"

"*Whatever* they want." After drawing a stuttered breath, she said, "They do it before you go on national service. They take turns. They make sure …" She broke off, pressing the back of her hand to her nose. "They make sure they don't get you pregnant, but they let you know who you belong to. They make sure they humiliate and degrade you just because they can. They do it to girls and boys."

As she stood in front of him, crying, Spike filled his lungs and released a long exhale. "My *god*. And Hugh's your chance to avoid that?"

"I *care* about him."

"I never said you didn't."

"Yes. We're going to live away from them. Hopefully, I'll find a way to get my brother and sister out before they're old enough to appear on the gangs' radar." She stared into the middle distance through glazed eyes. "Although, I didn't think I'd find a way to get myself out until I met Hugh."

Although Spike wanted better words, he only had, "I'm sorry. If I'd have known—"

"You've done more than enough. My hopes for a better life rest on Hugh getting through this alive. With you as a best friend, he has a better chance than most."

Spike half-smiled.

"What?"

"I'd not thought of Hugh as my best friend. But you're right; since getting here, we've definitely gotten close. I suppose he is. I used to think of Matilda in that way."

"But she's so much more, right?"

"*So* much more." Spike used the cloth to clean some cutlery before he handed it to Elizabeth. "Does he know about what you've been through?"

Elizabeth shook her head while biting down on her bottom lip. She finally managed, "It's a lot to get your head around."

The weight of the past few days pushing down on him, Spike

nodded. "Yeah. Well, don't worry, I won't say anything to him. It's your story to tell."

While Elizabeth sobbed, Spike thought about Matilda. The ray of hope. The reason to keep going. "Everything will work out."

For the first time since she'd walked into the hall, Elizabeth smiled. "I believe that. I really do. Thanks to you."

CHAPTER 22

The sharp knife burned as it cut into Spike's stomach. The first line of the five-pointed star, they'd surrounded him and pinned him to the ground. The one with the knife had an evil grin that caught the light. The glint of his blade. The grin turned into a grimace as he pushed down and started the next line.

Waking with a gasp, Spike saw the person over him and reached up, halting before he grabbed her throat. "Tilly?"

She pushed a finger to her lips. "Shhh!"

His heart pounding, his breaths uneven, Spike's head spun when he sat up too quickly. Matilda jumped down from his bed and silently beckoned him to follow her.

After he'd pulled his duvet back—the cold night biting into his exposed legs—Spike slipped from his bed, his bare feet landing on the chilled floorboards.

Once he'd gotten dressed, Matilda led the way from their dorm, moving with the grace of a highly skilled assassin. If only she could compete in the trials, they'd stand a much greater chance of one of them winning it.

When they stepped outside, their breaths visible in the chill air, Spike's tiredness left him. "It's the middle of the night."

Instead of responding, Matilda ran off across the national service area.

Nauseated from being awakened too soon, Spike gulped before he followed her, the dewy grass soaking his shoes, the ground uneven underfoot.

Matilda ran around the back of team Phoenix's dorm. The place had been abandoned for weeks now. A site no one visited. A ghost ship among an active fleet. But it hid them from whoever guarded the gate that evening. Someone from team Chupacabra.

After she'd peered around the side of the dorm, Matilda sprinted for the dining hall. It felt like Spike had only been in there a few minutes previously, talking to Elizabeth about what it had been like for her in the woodwork district.

Before Spike caught up to her, Matilda ran for the gym, vanishing around the back like she had the last time they climbed on its roof.

When Spike caught up to her again, he saw she'd made it halfway up the rungs on the back of the building. He followed, taking it slower than before because of the dew on the bottom of his shoes and his still mildly unresponsive limbs from having not yet properly woken up.

On top of the roof, Spike sat down and caught his breath, large clouds of condensation billowing from him. He looked at the training area on the other side of the wall. "They've finished the first two trials now. I wonder who's in the lead and what they've made them do so far."

"It's not like *you'll* ever find out. Not with the way you're going."

"Wha …? Huh?"

"When will you stop being a hero, Spike?"

"What?"

"Hugh, earlier. I heard about what happened."

"What? I should have left him?"

"You left me the other day when I was being attacked."

As much as he wanted to tell her it was because he knew he had no chance of getting to her in time, Spike shrugged. "I know you can look after yourself."

Red-faced and wide-eyed, Matilda clenched her jaw. She dragged a deep breath in through her nose and released a large cloud of condensation. It seemed to help, her words softening. "I just need to know we're pushing in the same direction."

"Hugh would have *died* had I not done something."

"What about Artan? What about the apprenticeship? What about *us*?"

"It's okay."

"How?"

"Bleach has told me I haven't jeopardised my chances of being the next apprentice."

"But what if you *had?* What then? You could have thrown it all away. And what about Max?"

"What about him?"

"While you're standing out for all the wrong reasons, he's standing out for all the right ones."

"I've killed more diseased than him."

"Only just, and he's proving to be much more reliable than you." A moment passed where she looked away from him as if to gather her thoughts. "I need you with me. I need to know you're going to be okay. That *we're* going to be okay."

Instead of replying, Spike looked at the training area again. The large and empty arena. The dorm all the cadets shared. What would it be like to share such a confined space with Ranger? He'd have to sleep with one eye open.

"Ranger could have stopped the diseased that attacked Hugh. He set it up. If you were there, you would have seen it. The diseased were running at Ranger, and instead of fighting them, he avoided them so they ran at Hugh."

Matilda opened her mouth and drew a breath, but Spike cut her off. "Like he removed the bolt from your sword."

"What?!"

"He's gunning for me. He's trying to make me fail by taking down the people I love."

"No." She shook her head. "Not even *he'd* do that."

"Just after you visited me at the gate the other night, Ranger turned up. He had a knife with him, which he put to my throat." Spike looked up and pointed to the cut on his neck. He heard Matilda gasp. "He threw the bolt at me that he'd removed from your sword."

"It could be a lie."

"It could be. But he definitely led the diseased to Hugh. And like Hugh saved your life by giving you his sword, I saved his. I would have done it even if I didn't feel indebted to him. That's what friends do."

Matilda's anger gave way to tears and she shook her head. "What's happening to me? I'm getting so focused on what I need to do, I'm not thinking about anyone else. This place is eating away at who I am."

"I think it's doing that to all of us."

"You should have told me about Ranger," Matilda said. While waving her finger between the two of them, she added, "This works both ways, you know? I need your help, but I want to give you mine. If he's against you, he's against us."

"This is the first time we've spoken since it happened."

While staring out over the training area, Matilda shifted so close to Spike their shoulders touched. A small amount of warmth in the chill night. He reached around and pulled her into him.

Another wave of tears left Matilda. "I'm *so* scared, Spike. So many things could go wrong. So many people have died. So many more will. I don't want to lose you. I don't want to leave Artan with my dad. I can't imagine a future where we live in different districts. Every time I close my eyes at night, I see the diseased bearing down on me. I don't think I've had one good night's sleep since this whole thing started."

Spike rocked Matilda while holding her tight.

"I feel like I'm losing my mind."

"We're nearly halfway there. We'll get through this, Tilly, I prom—"

Before Spike could finish his sentence, Matilda stretched up and kissed him. He tasted the salt of her tears. When she pulled away, she shook her head. "Don't say that."

"It makes everything better, you know."

While crying, she traced a heart on his forearm. "What does?"

"Knowing what's waiting for us at the end of this." Spike then saw movement below them. As much as he wished he didn't recognise the silhouettes, he'd know them both from a mile away. One tall and awkward, one short and stocky. "Ranger and Lance."

"Where are they going?"

It seemed obvious, but Spike waited for a few more seconds to be sure. "My dorm."

"Do you think they're looking for you?"

"They're up to something. I need to go and see what it is."

They kissed again before Spike eased off the roof, staring at his love while he backed down the ladder.

CHAPTER 23

Spike peered around the side of the dining hall, watching for signs of Ranger and his pet. The pair emerged a few seconds later, so he pulled back from view. As they drew close to him, he listened to their hushed tones and moved the opposite way around the large hall.

Lance had a louder voice, which made him easier to track even when Spike couldn't hear Ranger's whispered reply. And thank god he did; otherwise he wouldn't have known how to avoid the pair.

So dark, Spike didn't see the obstruction. A knee-high lump, he walked into it and fell, crashing down on the hard ground.

When the lump got to its feet and loomed over him, Spike let out a hard sigh. "Shit."

White light flashed through Spike's vision and fire torched his sinuses when Ranger punched him square on the nose. Blinded by his own watering eyes, he barked when someone drove a kick into his ribs. Another kick, the silhouette of Lance joined Ranger. Spike pulled his hands over his head to protect himself as the two boys went to work on him.

Adrenaline desensitised Spike to the attack. His head spun and the metallic taste of his own blood filled his mouth. As he felt his world fade, he nearly went with it. But he needed to do something before the two boys beat him senseless.

Seeing Lance's large feet close by, Spike waited for him to lift one so he could stamp down before he grabbed his standing leg and yanked hard. The tall boy fell, hitting Ranger on his way to the ground.

Spike jumped to his feet and clenched his fists. He saw the glint of a blade. Quicker than Ranger, he punched the boy on his thick chin. Once, twice … on the third time, Ranger dropped his knife and went down.

It looked like Lance might get up, so Spike kicked him in the stomach and winded the boy. With both of them on the ground, he took his chance and ran.

~

Like Matilda had done to him earlier that evening, Spike leaned over Hugh and nudged him. The boy opened his eyes with a gasp. He urged Hugh to keep his voice down by pressing a finger to his own lips. "Shh!"

While breathing heavily, Hugh's eyes shifted from side to side. As he sat up, his gasps slowed and his gaze settled. He reached out and touched Spike's face. "What happened to you?"

"Ranger and Lance."

"They dragged you out of bed?"

"I was outside already."

"Why?"

"That's not important. What matters is they were in here."

"You think they've tampered with our weapons?"

"That's my guess."

Hugh dressed in his clothes from the previous day before they both left the room.

Still short of breath from the kicking, his ribs tender, his face throbbing, Spike pulled down three swords while Hugh grabbed the other three. Before Hugh had a chance to speak, Spike led him outside and around the back of their dorm.

After putting the weapons down on the grass, Spike opened his mouth to speak, but the gruff clearing of a throat stopped him short.

Both boys turned around as one, and Spike stammered, "B-Bleach?"

Where Spike had seen anger on his team leader's face, he watched it change, his features falling slack. "What happened to you?"

"Ranger and Lance," Hugh said.

"Nice one, Hugh!"

"What?"

"Snitches get stitches, everyone knows that." When Hugh didn't reply, Spike returned his attention to Bleach. They were all in now. "I saw Ranger and Lance coming out of the dorm."

"You think they messed with the weapons?"

"They did it to Tilly's sword."

"You know that?"

"I can't prove it."

"Then you *don't* know it. So how did you end up in this state?"

"I ran into them outside."

"And what were you doing outside?"

While Bleach and Spike talked to one another, Hugh had picked up one of the swords. When it fell apart in his hands, it stopped their conversation dead.

Hugh lifted up the pieces and spoke while examining them. "They've gotten more advanced."

Bleach stepped closer to him. "How?"

A bolt in his pinch, Hugh found the moonlight so he could

show Bleach. "These scratches show it's been weakened with a tool of some sort. I'm guessing they were hoping they'd break out in the field when in use."

"And by then it's too late," Bleach said.

"Exactly."

"And it looks like an accident."

"Yep."

A deep inhale, Bleach pulled his thick and sleep-dishevelled hair back and held it there, his tired green eyes wide while he stared into the middle distance. "Well, we all know who Ranger is."

"What do you mean?" Spike said.

"He's Magma's son, which means if we want to get him kicked out of here, we need concrete evidence. I'm worried that not even Ranger's stupid enough to give us that."

"Isn't Spike's face evidence enough?" Hugh said.

Bleach shook his head. "No witnesses. Besides, what do we say? It happened when he was out with Tilly for a late night rendezvous."

"How do you know I was out with Tilly?"

After lifting an eyebrow at him, Bleach said, "So you'd have to admit to that, which would get you in trouble and exclude you from the trials."

A quickened pulse drove Spike's retort. "So we let him get away with it?"

"We plan against another sabotage, but I don't know what else we can do. Unless you have any suggestions?"

Spike didn't.

"I think," Bleach continued, "we need to make sure the weapons are hidden so they can't do this again, and we need to do everything we can to stay away from the evil little shit. My guess is he'll do something stupid soon enough. The best we can do is keep out of his way, and hopefully he'll expose himself."

"So we do *nothing*."

"Sometimes nothing is the best course of action. Now you two need to go to bed. Hugh, will you make sure you service the swords in the morning?"

Hugh nodded while gathering them up.

When Bleach put his arm around him, Spike winced. "I know it's hard to take what happened tonight and not react, but be smart. Beat him within the rules. Become the next protector and walk away with your head held high."

Throbbing all over from the kicking, Spike didn't reply. Instead, he twisted free from Bleach and followed Hugh back to their bedroom.

CHAPTER 24

Over a month had passed since Ranger tampered with team Minotaur's weapons. As Spike looked at the boy, soaked because of the rain, the boy still refused to look back. The way he'd left him and Lance the night of the fight had calmed them both down. If their relationship continued in this vein for the next few months and beyond, he'd take it, even though Magma had grown frostier with him since the run-in with his son.

Seven cadets had fallen in the past month; many of them caught unawares by the diseased while they worked on the wall. They didn't always have time to pull back within the perimeter and form a line. Sarah Banks from Bigfoot had perished, along with George Gonzalez, Alice Monroe, and Leanne Ostrander from team Chupacabra, Suzi Swing and Drew Peacock from Yeti, as well as Walt Jessie from Cyclops. But team Minotaur was still at one hundred percent, as was Dragon. Spike had witnessed every death and wanted to help in each one, but he couldn't save them all. Not if he wanted to save himself and those he most cared for.

The nod came from Magma to one of the guards, and both of them went to work, the loud and nerve-jangling ring of chains flying across wood. No matter how many times Spike stood there, the sound still ran tension through his back and sent his heart pounding. Who would die today? Would Matilda make it to the end? Not that Spike had told anyone, but he'd had several mornings over the past few weeks where he'd woken up paralysed by his fear. But until now, he'd managed to push through it. One foot in front of the other. One day at a time.

Just one diseased burst through the gap in the gates.

After Magma buried Jezebel in the creature's head, the teams of protectors marched out through the gates.

The barrow as heavy as ever, the wooden handles slick with the rain, Spike gritted his teeth to help him force the wheel forward through the softer ground.

The lethargic weight that turned Spike's bones to lead seemed to occupy all the cadets. They moved with a slow trudge and fanned out to their respective parts of the wall. Another long day ahead of digging, building, and keeping their eyes open for the diseased.

∽

WEEKS OF WORK HAD HARDENED SPIKE'S HANDS TO THE JOB. He picked the rough wet stones up and slid them into place in the wall. Hugh dug another empty grave nearby, loading Olga up with a supply of clay, which she mixed with grass she did her best to keep dry in the rain, and served it to Spike.

Before Bleach said anything, Spike sensed it. His team leader stood alert, staring out over the long grass in the direction of the ruined city. When he saw Bleach's hands shake as he fumbled for the horn around his neck, he dropped the brick he had in each hand and stood up.

The long grass swayed, the rain running almost horizontally in the heavy wind. At first Spike froze. He didn't believe what he saw. Then Bleach's horn sounded, his team leader shouting, "Horde! We've got a horde."

At least thirty of them no more than five hundred feet away. The grass would have hidden them for longer were there not so many, but a mob that large didn't do subtlety.

The horns of the team leaders called out, all of them shouting the same order. "Get inside the perimeter and hold your ground."

While drawing his sword, Spike ran inside the wall, checking Matilda came in too. Dragon were organised, Tank pulling them into a defensive line. But he could still go and be with her. Then he heard his name. "Spike!"

The rest of the cadets moved past Spike at a sprint. A stampede of bodies, the diseased in the long grass closed down on them. He heard his name again. "Spike."

"Hugh?" Although Spike couldn't see him.

"Help."

The diseased were getting closer. Should he go to Matilda?

"Spike! Help me."

For the briefest moment, Spike and Matilda made eye contact with one another. She nodded at him. She'd be okay. Hell, she'd probably do better than him.

Spike ran back outside the walls to see Hugh standing in the grave he'd dug. He should have been able to get out, but he stood frozen.

The shriek of the diseased grew louder. Now just a couple of hundred feet away. As much as Spike wanted to berate the boy, that would come later. For now, he reached down, took his large hand, and pulled him from the hole.

"Thank you," Hugh said.

Instead of responding, Spike shoved the boy in the direction of the other cadets. "Run, you fool."

Although he wanted to run faster, Spike kept Hugh ahead of him. The other cadets had already formed two short lines, and they watched the wall. The strong cadets were at the front, the weaker ones behind. Hugh joined the second line.

Fright's voice rang loud enough to be heard over the rain and the diseased's shrieks. "This is a horde. They happen. Don't break the line. Don't give them the chance to single us out. The only way to deal with this is as a unit. So listen to your orders and fight like you've never fought before."

The diseased yells came at them through several gaps in the wall.

Spike held his sword in a two-handed grip, tried to settle his breaths, and squinted into the rain as he listened to the creatures close down on them. They were ready; they could do this. Then he heard Hugh shouting for a second time.

"Where's Elizabeth?" His voice rose in pitch. "Elizabeth? Elizabeth?"

The first sign of something bursting through the wall came in the form of Ranger and Lance. No one had noticed either of them were gone. Damn shame they'd made it back. A moment later, Elizabeth ran in after them, her nose bloodied, her hair a dishevelled mess.

"Someone help her," Hugh shouted. "Please, someone help Elizabeth."

Before Spike could step from the line, Bleach clamped a strong hand on his shoulder. "Stay put!"

CHAPTER 25

Spike only saw Hugh's run to save Elizabeth when it got crudely halted by Bleach's elbow. The boy yipped, stumbled backwards while covering his nose with both hands, and fell to the ground.

As Ranger and Lance joined the line, the first of the diseased crashed into Elizabeth, its clumsy run ending in a collision of heads. The loud *crack* whipped around the space inside the walls. Elizabeth's eyes rolled back and her legs buckled. The diseased fell too.

The next creature—what looked to have once been a teenage boy—landed on top of the unconscious Elizabeth and tore a chunk from her arm. Blood ran from its eyes and mouth. It then jumped up and led the charge at the rest of the cadets.

Fright yelled, "Hold your ground and let them come to you."

And come to them they did. The diseased flooded in through the gaps in the walls like a plague. A cacophony of chaos shrieked as they closed in. They swiped at the air with their hands, and their jaws flapped.

Although Bleach had hit Hugh hard, he hadn't hit him hard enough to render him unconscious. The sound of his friend nearly broke Spike's concentration. But he couldn't do anything for his tears at that moment. Elizabeth was gone.

Shoulder to shoulder with his fellow cadets, Spike brought his sword down in a vertical hack, embedding it in the skull of the first diseased to get close. Only able to focus on his own battle, he tried to shut out the cries and grunts around him.

Spike stabbed the next one through the shoulder. The creature's cry rang so shrill it hurt his ears. The thing spun away from him, nearly yanking his sword from his grip.

Sweat mixed with rain and Spike blinked against its blinding assault while swinging at the next beast. The fight had opened gaps in their line. They needed the space to swing their swords.

"Keep going," Fright said. "Just keep fighting."

Another stab, followed by another one, Spike downed two more but killed neither. A moment to glance at the wall, he saw they were all inside the perimeter now. He killed the two he'd downed.

Over almost as quickly as it had begun, Spike panted while he looked at the bodies around him. Some of the cadets had fallen and already been slain. Fresh blood haemorrhaged from their eyes. Matilda looked okay. Tired, but okay.

A commotion to his right, Spike watched the team leaders surround Rich Marksman. He dropped his sword and held his hands up. "I'm fine; there's nothing wrong with me."

Despite the rain, Spike saw the sweat on his brow. His skin had turned paler than usual. His eyes were wide.

"Please," he said. "I've *not* been bitten."

As he said it, a red patch spread through his tracksuit near his abdomen. As he self-consciously reached for it, he said, "I caught myself on my own sword."

The team leaders closed in tighter around him. All of them had their swords raised.

"We'll wait," Juggernaut said. "If you don't turn, we'll believe you."

Maybe Juggernaut saw it when Spike did. The slightest reddening in Rich's eyes. Within a few seconds, a film of blood had covered them. Juggernaut clearly didn't need any more evidence. He sank the tip of his sword into Rich's face, pulling it out as the boy folded to the ground.

Spike turned his back on the dead cadet and walked over to Hugh. "I'm sorry, mate. I couldn't get to her in time. None of us could."

Hugh kept his eyes on the ground, his shoulders bobbing as his grief flooded out of him.

CHAPTER 26

The flickering fire threw dancing light across the fronts of their clothes as they stood in a small circle around it. Past eleven in the evening, but none of them could sleep after the day they'd had. Bleach, Hugh, Spike, Heidi, Olga, Max, and Matilda. Hugh had given Matilda permission to join them.

Spike and Matilda stood shoulder to shoulder, Hugh on Spike's left, but not quite as close. Like everyone else, Spike watched the fire. Both the warmth and the hypnotising sway of the flames gave him a focal point, the orange glow a blur through his tear-filled eyes.

They'd been there a few minutes before Bleach cleared his throat. "Elizabeth, you gave yourself in service to this great city. May your spirit watch over us as we grow and prosper. Know we won't forget you when Edin is liberated from the oppressive control of trying to live in a world where the diseased exist. Know you are the reason we'll get there."

When Spike glanced across at Hugh, he saw the boy locked in a trance. Red rings encircled his tired eyes. He looked like he'd run out of tears.

The lull lasted for just a few seconds before Hugh said, "I knew Elizabeth well. We spent a lot of time together."

While his friend spoke, Spike reached across and rubbed his back. He thought about what Elizabeth had told him in the dining hall. Hugh didn't know about the gangs, and what purpose would it serve now? He needed to think of his love at rest, not living with the torment the gangs had forced on her before she left for national service.

An ironic laugh, Hugh shook his head. "Neither of us had plans to be protectors or politicians. Maybe we were foolish, but we had an idea that we could both work in the labs and live on site together. Liz was a wonderful person. She was funny, sharp, cutting when she needed to be. She kept her personality close to her chest, but when you got to know her, she shone like the sun."

After a pause to get his breaths under control, Hugh said, "She would have been a wonderful mother and life partner. She had plans to be both. No doubt she would have ended up running the labs too. She could have done it all. She could have had freedom in our restricted city."

Because he stood so close to her, Spike reached out with his fingers and touched the back of Matilda's right hand.

"She'd still be alive if I was braver," Hugh said.

Spike looked at his friend.

"If I wasn't so focused on my fear, I would have seen she'd not made it back and been able to help her. I would have been able to get her away from Ranger and Lance."

"We don't know what happened on the other side of the wall," Bleach said.

"Oh, come on. We know *exactly* what happened. It's only that we can't prove it, and because of that, Ranger gets away with it again. The boy's evil, and were he not Magma's son, we'd have left him outside the gates weeks ago."

As much as Bleach looked like he wanted to reply, he kept it to himself.

"Either way," Hugh went on, "I was more concerned with looking after myself than helping her. That's on me. My cowardice is my cross to bear."

A quick glance at the others, all of them with tears in their eyes, Spike turned to Hugh. "This is what national service is. You shouldn't blame yourself for it."

"What would you have done if Matilda was in the same situation?"

Before Spike could reply, Matilda cleared her throat with a wet cough. "He would have let me fight my own battle. He knows the importance of at least one of us going back home alive."

As much as Spike wanted to contest it, he remained mute.

From the narrowing of his eyes, it seemed clear that Hugh saw right through him. "Whatever you would have done, I should have done more." He shook his head and walked away from the fire.

Heidi moved as if to go after him, but Spike grabbed her. "Don't. He needs time on his own."

The fire continued to dance and shimmy in the wind, flickering in Spike's peripheral vision as he watched his friend vanish into the darkness.

CHAPTER 27

Elizabeth had died nearly five weeks ago. Since the night around the fire, Hugh hadn't spoken a word to anyone. Spike had given up trying to engage him in conversation, but remained at his side whenever he could. He wanted to be available for him if he decided to open up.

They lined up outside the gates, only eighteen cadets left from the forty-two who had gathered in the same spot four and a half months previously. How many would be standing at the end of it all? Ranger remained, the short and squat boy standing next to his lanky sycophant, Lance. Many good rookies had gone before them, including Liz.

The protectors lined up in front of the gates in the same way they did every morning. Magma had thrown disdain at Spike again. But it didn't matter anymore. Too much else had happened since they'd been there. If Magma didn't like him, he could keep his resentment.

The rush of chains, the gates opening, and again, just one diseased outside, which Warrior dispatched.

Like he did every morning, Bleach said, "Don't take this as normal. It's happened enough for you to think this is the way it is now, but it *will* change. Make sure you're ready for it when it does."

All the while Bleach spoke, Hugh glared at him. The mole of a boy worked his jaw, his lips pursed as if he fought to keep his words back.

"Do you have a problem, boy?" Bleach said.

Hugh didn't reply. But he didn't look away either.

~

They'd woken up to a warm morning, but now they were halfway through the day and the sun had reached its zenith, Spike felt like he wanted to claw his own skin off to escape the heat. Sweat ran from every pore, his clothes sodden, his eyes stinging. At least his skin was resilient to the weather. When he looked at Hugh and the others in his team, he could almost see them blistering with every passing second.

Now he'd done a stint digging the grave and building the wall, Spike took his turn on guard with Max. A two-handed grip on his broadsword, it might have been hot, but at least he only had to stand there now.

The tall grass barely moved in the still day. Spike had a clear view over the top of the golden meadow all the way to the ruined city on the other side. On a day with a heavier breeze, he might not have seen it so soon, but when the grass moved slightly, he raised his sword.

Max tensed next to him, and Bleach said, "Is everything okay?"

Spike nodded at the patch in the meadow that moved slightly differently to the rest of it. "It doesn't look like a diseased though; it's not running."

After walking over so he stood closer to them, Bleach said, "What, then?"

"An animal?" Max said.

Spike smiled. "Dinner?"

Bleach shrugged. "Maybe."

A white flag then burst from the grass, the fabric limp.

Spike, Max, and Bleach stepped back as one.

The flag remained aloft as the carrier continued towards them.

A few seconds later, a woman emerged. She had black hair that stuck out in every direction as if she'd been dragged through the field. Dirt stained her face, and the whites of her eyes stood out against her grubby skin. Her mouth hung slightly open and her lips were cracked. She had two batons of wood strapped to her body, batons made from snapped branches, batons covered in the blood of what Spike could only assume to be the diseased. The end of each one had been sharpened to a point.

The boom of Bleach's voice made Spike jump. "Stay where you are!"

The woman continued forwards as if she hadn't heard him.

"I *said* stay where you are. Don't move."

"Something's not right with her," Spike said.

"You can say that again."

"I mean, I don't know if she's a threat to us."

"Do you think she's deaf?" Max said.

When Bleach twitched as if to move forward, Spike grabbed his arm.

"What are you doing, boy?"

"I'm not sure she understands you."

"What?"

"I don't think she's been bitten, and I don't think she means us harm, but I don't think she knows what you're saying either." While he watched her, Spike thought about the sound outside the gate when he'd done guard duty weeks back. The sound of the diseased being silenced. The sound of steps that belonged to something other than one of the vile creatures. They'd sounded human. "I think she's the reason so few diseased have been outside the gates in the morning."

"She's killing them all on her own?"

A shrill scream, the grass parted, and a diseased leaped at the woman. In one fluid movement, the woman dropped her flag, drew her makeshift batons, and drove two hard whacks against the creature's head, one with each weapon. As the diseased fell, she spun her batons around and drove them into the creature's eyes with pinpoint accuracy.

"Okay, William," Bleach said while he stared at the woman. "I'm going to trust you on this."

After taking the diseased down, the woman panted, her wild eyes even wider on her dirty face. She lifted her white flag again.

"See," Spike said. "She means us no harm."

"So what do we do with her?" Bleach turned to the woman. "What do you want from us?"

For the first time, the woman replied, but she didn't use words Spike had ever heard before. "What's she saying?"

"I don't know."

Max maintained his grip on his weapon, but he'd relaxed his stance. "Whatever it is, she has a lot to tell us."

The woman barely paused for breath, her words falling from her mouth in an endless stream of what sounded like gibberish.

"I think we need to look after her," Spike said. "I think she's been out here for a while and she needs our help. We should take her in. I think she can tell us things about the outside world that we don't know. If we ever work out how to understand her, that is."

Bleach nodded. "I'll take her in to be looked after, and we can let the politicians decide what to do with her."

The mention of politicians sank dread through Spike. But what else could they do? It seemed like the most appropriate course of action.

Spike watched his team leader walk out to meet the woman. He put his arm around her and spoke soft words that she probably didn't understand. "It's okay, love, we're going to look after you. It's over now. You're safe."

As the pair passed Spike and Max back towards the gates leading to the national service area, Spike shook his head while watching her. "Why do I feel like we've just sealed that woman's doom?"

CHAPTER 28

"I can't believe we only have four weeks left in this place."
It had gotten to the point where Hugh wouldn't even look at Spike when he talked, let alone reply to him. Nearly two months of silence since Elizabeth had died. But Spike thought he knew his short friend well enough to know when he did and didn't want him around. And what else would they do today?

"And we were lucky to win the final Monday off. I'm exhausted."

Together, Spike and Hugh stood near the dining hall. They watched the few remaining cadets gathering to go out for the day. "There's so few of us left. At one point, I wondered if any of us would make it through national service."

A slight wince, Hugh looked like he might say something, but every time Spike expected him to talk, he didn't.

"And what do you think they've done with that woman?" Spike watched Matilda make her way down to the gates, most of her team with her—minus the fallen Abbie Shrink. "I don't know what she was saying or where she was from, but it means there's something more than ruin out there, right? I mean, I always thought there was, but she's evidence of it. It's been two weeks since she appeared." Although Spike didn't say it, he thought about the woman being evicted through the back of the city. Those emptying their chamber pots wouldn't know anything about her, so it wouldn't be suspicious. Rather than the ray of hope she could have brought to Edin, she might well have become entertainment for a few short minutes. And he'd never know if they'd done it or not. Maybe he'd ask his dad when he got back. He could probably describe her to him. Maybe she would have fought the creatures. Unlike most of Edin's residents, who had grown soft since their national service, she had it in her.

During his time there, Spike hadn't often let his mind wander to his parents. How had they been over the past five months? How much had his mum gotten on his dad's nerves? No doubt she'd barely slept for the entire time, worrying about whether he'd be coming home or not, expecting every visitor to be bringing bad news to their door.

The snorting laugh of Lance Cull dragged Spike's attention behind him. Hugh remained staring out at the gates.

"Ladies," Lance said and laughed again.

Although Spike watched the pair, he said nothing. But when Ranger moved close to Hugh, he stepped forward to protect his friend.

The same thick brow, the same condescending sneer, the same face that longed to be punched, Ranger looked Hugh up and down. "Still mute, then, boy?"

A slight pinch at the sides of his eyes, Hugh continued to stare down at the gates.

"Why don't you two run along?" Spike said. "The gates will be opening soon. I know you get a free ride because of who your dad is, but you need to at least try to be a passable cadet, right?"

If Spike's words bothered Ranger, he didn't show it. Cruelty swirled in the darkness of his glare, and the slightest hint of a smile played with the edges of his mouth. If he leaned any closer to Hugh, they'd be touching. "Unlike you, Elizabeth had plenty to say."

Hugh's focus shifted from the gates to Ranger.

When Lance stepped closer to Hugh, Spike shoved him back. The two boys glared at one another, but Lance quickly yielded, dropping his attention to the ground.

"She had a lot of fight in her too."

"That's *enough*," Spike said.

"Lance and I kicked her as hard as we could, and she still wanted to get up. I had to break her nose before she stayed down."

"I said *that's enough!*"

"Why did you leave her on her own outside the walls anyway?"

"I didn't!"

The words forced Spike back a step. The first thing Hugh had said in weeks.

"You can thank Spike for her demise."

"*What?*" Spike said.

"Well, it's all part of the plan, isn't it? Get to you through those you love. I noticed the late night rendezvous you and Elizabeth had in the dining hall. Have you told Hugh about that?"

Hugh's face fell slack when he looked at Spike.

"She helped me with the dishes when I had to clean them. She wanted to thank me for keeping you alive when Ranger tried to set the diseased on you."

It didn't matter why she'd gone to see Spike, just the fact that she'd been and he hadn't told Hugh wasn't helping the situation.

"You looked awfully cosy," Lance said.

A balled fist and clenched jaw, Spike turned on the lanky boy. "You're well out of your depth. I'd wind my neck in if I were you."

After a glance at the gates, Ranger turned back to Hugh. "You should have seen the fear in her eyes. It was wonderful. She begged for help, you know? She even said your name."

Deep breaths worked through Hugh, his chest rising and falling with them.

"But she probably should have called for Spike, don't you think?"

Hugh's tense body sagged and tears filled his eyes.

Both Lance and Ranger laughed. Ranger winked at Spike. "Anyway, gotta get outside the walls today. Let's see what I can do to team Dragon while I'm out there."

Two large arms restrained Spike when he lunged at Ranger. Bleach's deep voice said, "Piss off, Ranger, you entitled little brat."

After blowing Bleach a kiss, Ranger turned his back on the three of them and walked off.

"Are you boys okay?" Bleach said.

Before Spike replied, Hugh walked in the opposite direction.

"I'll take that as a no, then, shall I?"

Although Spike made to follow Hugh, Bleach held onto him. "I know Ranger's a prick, but you and Max are level pegging for a place in the trials. Don't do anything stupid that'll jeopardise that." He then released his grip.

CHAPTER 29

Maybe Hugh thought it would be the last place Spike would look. And he was right. Why would Spike keep searching when he'd found the object of his hunt? But he'd certainly checked nearly everywhere else he could think of first, spending most of the morning wandering in search of his friend. Very few cadets chose to go anywhere near the hole.

The hot sun beat down on Spike as he approached his friend, sweat soaked from how much walking he'd done. He tried to keep his focus on Hugh rather than thinking about what lay behind the wooden wall. Or rather, what existed beneath them at that moment. No wonder Ranger had lost the plot. A second visit so soon after the first seemed like a brutal punishment—not that he had much sympathy for the arrogant prick.

When Hugh looked up and pressed against the ground as if to get to his feet, Spike raised a hand at him. "Hear me out. Please."

It looked like apathy more than anything that made Hugh sink back where he sat.

Spike dropped down next to him, his back to the wooden wall. "Elizabeth came to see me when I had to clean up the dining hall.

She said she wanted to thank me, but I think she also wanted to talk."

As had been their relationship for the past few weeks, Spike hoped Hugh would speak, but filled the silence when he didn't. "She wanted to tell me how much you meant to her. How much she loved you and how excited she was about the plans you had for a future together."

"She did?"

"Yeah. She said you'd work and live on site at the labs. That you were kind and she loved you for that."

"So what are you not telling me?" Hugh said.

"I don't know if it's my story to tell."

"It's not like you can ask her permission. Or upset her. If it will help me understand, then it's your story to tell."

"Did you know the woodwork district controlled by gangs?"

"No."

"I didn't either, but apparently it is. Horrible, nasty gangs that run the district and threaten to cause chaos in the entire city if the politicians or guards intervene. There's enough of them to bring Edin to its knees."

"So what do they want?"

"Elizabeth told me that when you come back from national service, you belong to them for a few years. They do what they want with you. It doesn't sound pretty."

"When you say *what they want* …?"

Spike nodded. "They'd done it to Elizabeth before she left. They do it to the girls and boys. They break them to shame them and remind them who they belong to. Elizabeth had a star cut into her from the gangs."

"Where?"

"On her stomach."

"And that's what Ranger saw her doing? Showing you that?"

"I can only assume."

"So why didn't she tell me?"

"She would have, and she planned to, but she didn't want you to think she was only with you because you'd free her from the gangs. She cared about you."

As Hugh looked out over the national service area, chaos swirled in his brown-eyed glare. A second later, the glaze of tears spread across them. His breaths grew deeper, his nostrils flaring. A slight buckling of his bottom lip, he bit down on it and frowned. When he spoke, his voice trembled. "I miss her so much, Spike."

Spike shifted closer to his friend and put an arm around his shoulder. "I know you do, mate. I know."

While Hugh cried in his embrace, Spike said, "It's good that you're talking again. It's important to let it out."

"I have to be better."

"Huh?"

"Liz died because I needed you to save me." The next wave of grief robbed him of his words for a few seconds. "If I'd have been able to look after myself out there, I would have been able to keep an eye on her. We were in the same team. She was right beside me when we saw the horde."

"What happened wasn't your fault."

"But she was right beside me. I could have done something. I know nothing will bring her back, but I need to get better. I need to be stronger. Will you help me?"

"Of course I will." Spike hugged Hugh tighter. "Of course I will."

A red-faced Olga appeared a few seconds later, panting and glistening with sweat. She forced her words through her heavy breaths. "Spike ... we've been looking ... for you."

A cold chill sank through Spike as he let go of Hugh and sat up straighter. "What's happened?"

Tears in her eyes, Olga shook her head. "I'm sorry."

"*What's happened?*"

"Team Dragon."

The air left Spike's lungs.

"They've fallen. All of them."

CHAPTER 30

A noise he didn't recognise as his own came from Spike. A deep donkey bray. The sound of his soul splitting.

When he'd finished, Olga stepped back from him and winced. "Bleach wants you to stay here with us. Sorry."

"What do you mean *he wants me to stay here?*"

"He said there's nothing that can be done at the moment, and he thinks you should keep yourself away from other people for a short time while you let it sink in."

His world spiralling, Spike rocked where he sat and shook his head. "So Tilly's *dead?*"

"She ran."

The words cut through the chaos. "What?"

"She ran. Team Dragon got attacked by a horde, which cut off their retreat. The rest of them were taken down, but Tilly managed to get away. She lost her sword fighting the diseased."

"So she couldn't continue fighting?"

"No."

"Well, of course she ran."

"She headed for the ruined city."

Although he'd heard Olga's words, the information scrambled

in Spike's head. While holding the side of his face, he said, "I just need to get this straight in my mind. No one saw her die?"

"No."

"So she's still alive?"

When Olga didn't reply, Spike looked up at her, her brow pinched in the middle. "Sorry, that's not a fair question. But no one's seen her die?"

"No."

"Okay. I'll stay here like Bleach has asked, but I'd like to be left alone with Hugh."

"Bleach will kick my arse if I leave you unguarded."

Spike's words crackled when he said, "I'll kick your arse if you don't."

A momentary glance at Hugh, Spike noticed his friend nod at Olga, who shrugged. "I'm sorry, Spike. I truly am."

Before she took off, Spike said, "Olga?"

The short girl turned back around. "Did Ranger have anything to do with it?"

She shook her head. "Not according to everyone out there. It was a freak attack, and because there's so few cadets now, they couldn't regroup to defend against them."

While swallowing the lump in his throat, Spike watched Olga walk away before he shook his head. "She's not dead."

"How do you know?"

"I just do."

"But what—?"

"I need to believe she's still alive, Hugh. I'll believe it until I *know* she's not. It's the only way I can move forwards." Despite the heat of the day, Spike shivered.

"And what about the promise you've made her?" Hugh said.

"What? To give up on her? To not help her when she needs me?"

"You know what the promise was, Spike. You promised you'd

be there for Artan if she couldn't. You now *need* to be a protector so you can get him out of his district and away from their dad. You go after her and they'll drop you from the trials. If she survived, she'll be back."

"But what if she can't come back for some reason?"

"Like what?"

"She doesn't have a sword, for one."

"If you stay inside the gates, you have a chance to be the next protector and look after her little brother like you promised. You have a chance of being the next protector for when she comes back. She's tough. If she's still alive, she's coming back. You go outside and you throw everything away. You might not find her. And you might not return yourself. Think about Artan."

"But what if she needs me out there? Without my help, she might die. I can bring her back so she'll be alive to look after Artan herself."

"And you'll miss out on the trials."

"Being a protector means nothing without her; don't you get that? And she's alive still. I *know* she is."

"How?"

Spike made a fist with his right hand and tapped it against his chest. "I can feel her in here. I need to help her come back. It's the right thing to do. She's the one best equipped to look after Artan, not me."

Although Hugh looked like he wanted to say more, Spike shook his head to stop him. "I can't give up on her. Not if there's a chance."

Hugh sighed and nodded. "I know you can't. Just promise me you'll think it through before you do anything rash."

Spike got to his feet. "I need some time."

"I understand. But what about what Bleach said?"

"Screw what Bleach said. Oh, and if you need someone to help you train while I'm away, ask Olga. She's a warrior."

CHAPTER 31

As they passed the dining hall on their way to the gates, Spike noticed Hugh yawn. "Sorry, man, I couldn't sleep a wink last night. I didn't mean to keep you awake."

Hugh nodded and yawned again. "It's fine. I should have moved to the bed beneath Max sooner. I can imagine it must have been hard for you to rest. And where did you go in the middle of the night? I thought you were trying to get outside the wall."

Because it would have been too obvious to take a backpack with him, Spike had filled a long cloth bag with rough bread he'd stolen from the dining hall. He currently had it tied around his waist beneath his clothes, his top baggy enough to conceal it. When he didn't reply, Hugh's kind eyes narrowed. Although he looked like he wanted to say something, he let it go.

The rest of Minotaur too close to them, Spike didn't want to jeopardise his plan by talking about it. Instead, he looked at the barrows and the few cadets who'd made it to the gates before them. The bright sun dazzled him and he'd already started to sweat in the fierce glare of it. There were so few there compared to how many had gone out on the first day. The absence of two entire teams left huge gaps in the gathered ranks. After shifting closer to Hugh as they walked, Spike spoke so only his friend heard him. "She's alive; I know she is."

"So you're set on doing it?"

Spike nodded.

"Please reconsider. I hate to be the one to say it, but there's no way Matilda—"

"Then don't. You can believe what you like, but that doesn't mean *I'm* going to. You might think you're the voice of reason, but you're only the voice of *your* reason. I've spent the last few months going against my better judgement and have watched people like Mercy die when I should have helped. The only time I went against their advice, I saved your life. Experience has taught me to listen to my better judgement. I'm not seeking anyone's counsel on the best course of action anymore. As my best friend, I wanted you to know what I'm going to do. That's all."

"But what if you're wrong?"

"What if I'm right? You, more than anyone, know what it's like to lose someone. If there's a chance she's still alive, that's enough. I'd rather die trying than give up."

"I've never had a friend before—a friend or a girlfriend. Don't make me lose both so close to one another."

"I'll come back, I prom—"

"Don't!"

It derailed Spike, his eyes burning with the start of tears. "Matilda wouldn't ever let me make promises either. Oh, and, Hugh, can you please tell Max I said well done. He deserves to be the next apprentice."

~

Spike and Hugh headed for their usual spot, but before they could settle, the team leaders herded all the cadets closer to one another. Standing shoulder to shoulder, the weight of Team

Dragon's absence hung heavy in the air. Almost a third of the cadets gone in one day. It felt like the group had lost a collective limb. Yet he could feel Matilda like an amputee could feel the wriggling fingers on an absent hand. Although, it was more than just memory; Matilda was still alive.

Placing his barrow down, Spike looked at the protectors. They limbered up, stretching as they prepared for an onslaught. All of them save Magma. He stood dead still, staring at the gates as if his glare would force them apart. For the first time in weeks, the fierce protector hadn't glowered at him. Maybe he saw the loss of team Dragon as punishment enough. And what did Spike care now anyway? If he tried to find his love, he had no chance of getting into the apprenticeship trials, so it wasn't like he needed to appease the temperamental arsehole anymore.

While twirling his skull ring, stress cramps running through his stomach, Spike turned to Hugh one last time. Instead of looking back, Hugh stared straight ahead, his eyes covered in a glaze of unshed tears.

For some, a gut feeling wasn't enough to risk your life. For Spike, it was all he had. Every time he'd had an instinct to act and hadn't, something bad had happened. Something preventable. But how could he expect Hugh to understand or trust that? For him, this was goodbye.

When Sarge limped across the front of the gates, he walked as if his boots were made from lead. Wearing a grisly frown, he finally came to a halt in front of everyone.

Spike reached back and touched the handle of his sword. Despite checking several times already, he looked down at his boots to make sure the laces were tied tightly. He subtly adjusted the fabric bag strapping the bread to his stomach. Although he felt Ranger's attention on him, he ignored it. He had far more important things to deal with.

At the sound of Sarge's gravelly voice, Spike snapped his head up.

"You little losers have less than a month left. You're on the home stretch. It would be nice if at least some of you cross the finish line. With your numbers as diminished as they are, that makes you even more vulnerable out there. Keep your wits about you."

Spike leaned across and rubbed Hugh's back. It would be nice to leave him on good terms.

Although Hugh didn't look, Spike saw his Adam's apple bob, the tears in his eyes swelling.

Holding his hand in the air, Sarge gave the order. "Open the gates."

Because Magma normally did it, Spike could have sworn he saw the scowling man's scowl deepen.

The rushing sound of chains over wood. For the first time in weeks, the call of the diseased responded in kind. Now the strange woman had been taken in, the numbers outside were increasing again.

Several heavy thuds crashed into the opposite side of the gates. Screams and yells, shrill and chaotic, melded with fists driving a frenzied tattoo of blows against the barrier keeping them from their prey.

The gap in the gates opened wide enough for atrophied and pale limbs to snake through. Crush stepped forward with her sword. Her huge arms bulged, and when a head poked through the gap, she yelled and swung at it. The wet crack sent a wash of weakness through Spike's knees. How many times would he have to do that before he found Matilda? Then it hit him. What if Matilda had been turned and she was among the mob outside?

The gates shook, the tops swaying under the pressure as if a hurricane crashed against them. As the chains screamed their intention, Spike tried to regulate his breaths.

Distracted by the diseased and searching for Matilda, Spike only noticed Sarge walking towards him when he got to just feet away.

"William, you're coming with me today. We don't want you out in the field because of what happened with team Dragon."

Another chorus of screams charged the diseased. Warrior, Hulk, and Axle had joined the battle. Wet hacks and squelches, the diseased fell like they always fell. As things became more chaotic, Spike focused harder to see if Matilda fell too.

"Did you hear me, William?"

Instead of turning to Sarge, Spike glanced at Hugh. His friend returned his gaze. The bright sun caught the glistening tracks of tears running down his face, and he dipped him an almost imperceptible nod.

"William!" Just a few feet separated Spike and Sarge.

The gates were halfway open. Many of the diseased had fallen, and none of them were Matilda. The ruined city lay on the horizon.

While watching the fight, Spike stepped away from his barrow and nodded at Sarge. "Okay, let's go."

Sarge paused and tilted his head to the side. A few seconds later, he said, "Fine. Good." He turned around as if to lead Spike away from the gates.

After winking at Hugh, Spike bolted, breaking away from the cadets and slipping through the line of team leaders.

While he ran at the gate, Sarge called after him, "William!"

His heart pounding, just the protectors stood between Spike and freedom—a lot of protectors. The shrill calls of the diseased drowned out Sarge's orders.

Spike halted as Magma raised Jezebel. He waited for him to bring her down. Maybe Spike distracted him, because the fierce protector hit the beast's shoulder instead of cracking its skull like he normally did. As it fell, Spike made a break for it. The creature needed finishing off. Magma would be too busy with it to stop him.

Swords and axes swung, Spike weaving through them as the metallic and vinegar reek of diseased blood tainted the air. All the while, he scanned the wretched faces of the creatures for his love.

Crush remained at the front of the protectors standing in the middle of the open gates. A pile of bodies lay around her, and more diseased came through at them. The gates continued to open. The chains continued to sing.

Spike stepped on one of the fallen and leaped forwards. He led with his right boot, kicking a diseased in the chest and sending it stumbling back into the others.

A small gap, Spike darted through it, the hot and rancid funk of the creatures in the summer air damn near choking him. His first step turned on the fallen body of a diseased, but his second found solid ground. One of the downed creatures reached out and clipped the back of his ankle, sending him stumbling several steps before he regained his balance and quickened his pace.

Now free from them, Spike looked behind as he ran, the tightly wrapped sack of bread rubbing against his stomach. From what he could see, Matilda wasn't in their number.

Gasping to fill his lungs, Spike dropped his head and sprinted with all he had.

When he passed through the new wall, Spike turned to face Edin. Four diseased were chasing him. He unsheathed his sword.

One ran quicker than the rest. Using its momentum against it, Spike speared its face with the tip of his weapon, burying it into the centre of its head. He kicked it in the chest, knocking it from his blade in time to face the next two.

Dodging the first one's windmilling attack, the creature stumbling past him and falling into the long grass, Spike then brought his weapon down on the skull of the third. A moist crunch and his sword stuck in the creature's head.

Once he'd wriggled his blade free, Spike swung it at the last of the group, removing its left leg at the knee and sending it crashing into the other one he'd knocked down.

Spike didn't give them a moment, stabbing both of them through the head while they lay on the ground.

Heavy breaths rocked Spike's frame as he watched the gates. Bleach led a charge in his direction. His usually immaculate brown hair bounced as he ran, his face red and glistening with sweat. "William!"

After watching him for a second longer, Spike turned his back on him and Edin and sprinted towards the ruined city. Deep breaths helped him find his rhythm as he pulled in the smell of fresh grass and opened a lead on those who thought to chase him. The ruined city as his goal, whatever happened, he would find Matilda.

CHAPTER 32

When he burst from the long grass, fighting to pull air into his lungs, Spike stopped and looked behind again. If anyone had followed him, they'd clearly given up the chase. And in the scorching heat, he couldn't blame them. Sweat turned his body slick, and his saliva had turned into a thick paste that he couldn't swallow. He should have brought some water. But where would he have hidden it? And at least he'd made it. Whatever it took, he'd find his love.

While resting on his knees, Spike hunched over and continued to regain his breath. Despite his hammering heart and burning muscles, the ruins took his attention. They stretched for miles both in depth and width. Large broken stones like none he'd seen before—not even in the wall—littered the ground. What looked like it had once been a road of black rock ran through the city. Tufts and patches of grass had ripped cracks into it like scars.

Many of the buildings were made from brick and large grey stone. Skeletal metal bars jutted from the structures like broken fingers, snapped and pointing at awkward angles, reaching out as if with the intent of blinding someone. If only they knew how to erect structures like this in Edin. Instead of spreading outwards, they could grow into the sky. So many things had been lost to time. Forgotten techniques and technologies they might never rediscover.

Sweat ran into Spike's eyes, which he wiped away again, his entire body rocking with his deep breaths as he recovered from the run. The city might have stretched for miles, but he'd find Matilda. For a moment he forgot himself and cupped his hands to his mouth, nearly shouting her name. If he was to find her in the maze of ruins, he'd have to do it as quietly as possible. The diseased knew the place better than he did. They had every advantage.

The densely packed derelict city ahead of him, Spike looked behind one last time. Over one hundred protectors would be on him soon.

The rich smell of foliage around him, Spike looked at the vines and moss coating many of the devastated buildings. The broken structures loomed over him, but there had been a time where they would have stretched much taller. How high had the tallest one stood in its full glory?

After just a few steps, the snap of popping glass raced at him through the ruined streets. His hand on the hilt of his sword, Spike bit down on his bottom lip as he slowly drew it from its sheath. He might have recovered from the run, but as he stood there, waiting for whatever made the noise, his heart sped and his breathing quickened again.

When a diseased walked around the corner—its frame slumped as if it were being held up by a string attached to the top of its spine—Spike tightened his grip on his sword. What had once been a man, it had black trousers with a long tear running down the thigh. It revealed its shrivelled penis, the pathetic thing jiggling with its tired steps.

It took for the creature to move several paces closer to Spike, its attention still on the ground, for Spike to clear his throat. The thing's face snapped up. It glared at him through crimson eyes. Its jaw fell and it hissed as if the sound came from its stomach.

The smell of rancid vinegar wafted towards Spike, and bile lifted up in his dry throat. He tasted the thing on the back of his tongue. A mess all around him, he twisted his feet to both widen his stance and sure his footing. He had to hold the line and let it come to him.

But before it could run, Spike heard a scream to his right. Spinning around, he saw a second diseased just feet away. A panicked swing, but it struck true; he removed the beast's head in one manoeuvre.

Before he had a chance to set himself, the first diseased crashed into him, sending him and his sword flying. They both fell to the ground, Spike's right shoulder landing on a large rock, white-hot pain tearing through his back.

Spike gasped as he wrestled with the squirming diseased. The skinny yet strong creature writhed on top of him, making up for its light weight with frenzied movement, further smothering him with its foetid reek.

Retching from the stink of decomposition, Spike held the beast back and stared into its dark mouth. Half its teeth were missing, and the others were so rotten they looked like they'd remain in his skin if it bit him.

While keeping a strong grip on its narrow shoulders, Spike held the thing at arm's length, his entire body shaking from the effort.

The diseased screamed again, so loud it drove needles into Spike's eardrums. The others would hear and soon there would be more. His strength threatening to give, he yelled and rolled the creature off him, kicking it away with both feet.

Even as Spike looked for his sword, he heard the creature scrabble upright. No time to find his weapon, he grabbed a brick instead.

Turning to see the beast swing, Spike ducked it, the creature's shriek rattling off the walls around them. When it charged again, he launched the brick. It smashed into the centre of the creature's face, halting its momentum and driving it backwards.

Before it could get up, Spike ran over to it, grabbed a two-foot-square piece of the black road, and dropped it on its head. Somewhere between a crunch and a moist pop, it turned the beast limp.

While fighting for breath, Spike spotted his sword. He stumbled over, lifted it from the ground, and quickly untied his bag of bread from his waist. At this rate, it wouldn't be edible for long.

A second or two to compose himself, his bag now strapped to his back, Spike heard the cry of more diseased, and his entire frame sank. Even if Matilda was in this city, how long would he last against an army of diseased? Was he chasing a dream? Should he have run from the gates in the first place? He could go back now. Sure, he'd get a scolding, but why had he come here? He needed more than hope to get him through. But he knew she was in the ruins somewhere. If he ignored it, he'd never forgive himself. And what would life be like without her?

Overwhelmed by the choice, he looked at the many paths in front of him. After one final breath, Spike forced himself to move and broke into a jog, heading deeper into the ruined city and in a different direction to the noisy diseased.

CHAPTER 33

Spike moved at a steady jog, watching the ground as he ran. The scatterings of hard debris would break an ankle the second he lost his focus. The sound of the diseased remained on his tail. He'd been running for at least twenty minutes, and he still had no idea where to look for Matilda.

Because he couldn't run forever, Spike slowed to a walk to catch his breath. If he was Matilda, where would he go? When he looked up, the conversation he'd had with her weeks ago on the roof of the gym came flooding back. The ruins on the steep hill. "Of course." He smiled. "I'm coming for you, Tilly." The smile vanished when he heard the shriek of the diseased. They were getting closer.

Other than the scuffle of shifting rubble beneath his steps, Spike made very little sound as he ran. It allowed him to listen to the beasts on his tail. Could they smell him? However they tracked him, they clearly weren't giving up. The ruins on the hill were too far away for him to get to. He needed a better plan in the meantime.

When Spike rounded the next corner, he saw the tall ruins of what must have once been a monster of a tower. Its top now a jagged point, it looked like a giant had reached down and snapped it off. Yet it still stood at least ten storeys high. A corpse of what it used to be, the walls were wrapped in vines, and empty holes sat where there had once been windows. The sounds of the diseased getting louder, he stared at it for a few seconds. *It'll work.*

Just a few feet from the entrance, the screams closer than ever, Spike ducked inside, the floor as treacherous as the rest of the city.

Although the first level stretched away from him with the potential for places to hide, Spike ran for the next floor, the old stone staircase bending in the middle and turning back on itself. He turned again and headed for the second.

The heavy pant of several diseased entered the building below.

Spike turned and ran for the third floor, but when he got halfway up, he skidded to a halt. A gap from where the stairs had collapsed prevented him from going any farther. It stretched too wide to jump, and he had nothing to hold on to if he wanted to climb across.

The vibration of the diseased chased him up the stairs. He looked down the gap in the middle to see at least ten of them, maybe even more. They were still on his tail and they weren't slowing down.

CHAPTER 34

When the mob reached the point where Spike had been between the second and third floors, he waited and listened. Their snarls and hisses were half-hearted and confused. They'd lost him and they knew it. They must have followed his sound rather than scent; otherwise they'd have smelled him by now. His arms shook from clinging onto the vines on the outside of the building. While holding his breath, he slowly climbed backwards down them.

Every vine Spike grabbed felt like it could come away in his grip, but they held. Years of melding with the ruined architecture, they covered the old tower like a second skin. Maybe they even kept the thing standing, the symbiosis of entropy.

The sounds of the diseased remained between the second and third floors. Their conference consisted of snaps, snarls, and groans. Could they communicate with one another? Probably not. They seemed like the ultimate selfish being: driven by a single-minded desire to destroy. Once they'd turned their prey, they returned to their lives of solitude.

When he got to the first-floor window, the vines thinned too much for him to continue his climb. Spike peered in. As he craned his neck—his body shaking with fatigue—he saw the creatures. They looked to be waiting for a sign as to his whereabouts. Sweating, he slowly stepped back in through the window and onto the first floor. His heart in his mouth, he listened to the creatures above. They still hadn't twigged.

Spike walked on tiptoes down the stairs, doing his best to keep his breathing even as he made slow progress towards the ground floor. Twitching spasms ran through his legs, daring him to run, but he fought against the urge.

At the bend in the stairs halfway between floors, Spike looked up through the middle. The creatures remained in the same spot. How long would they wait? Did they only respond to sound, conserving energy until they had something to chase?

At the bottom of the stairs, Spike looked back up again. He'd done it. So it must be sound they chased. As long as he kept the noise down, he'd be fine.

When Spike turned to face the exit, he froze. An involuntary gasp left him to see the creature in the doorway. The beasts above fell silent before screams assaulted him in stereo, from in front and from two floors up. The diseased in front ran at him while those above thundered down.

In one fluid movement, Spike drew his sword, brought it around, and hacked into the neck of the creature in the doorway. It distorted its scream and it fell, but he hadn't killed it. He didn't have time to kill it.

Dust shaking from the staircase above, Spike jumped the grabbing arm of the creature he'd wounded, and burst back out into the city. Too many to fight, he dipped his head and ran.

CHAPTER 35

Because he didn't want to lead the diseased to his destination, Spike spent the day losing them. He'd entered many buildings one way and exited another, weaving an untraceable escape from the monsters. It had taken several hours, but when he stopped—his breaths ragged and his throat so dry it bit a sharp pinch every time he swallowed—he listened. Nothing followed him. For the first time that day, nothing followed him.

A small building close by, Spike saw the doorway blocked with fallen debris. Like many of the buildings in the city, it had vines crawling up its walls. The top missing like with so many others, he climbed the vines. Before he descended the other side, he looked up at the ruins on the hill, the strong sun setting behind them. He'd get there tomorrow. "Hold on, Tilly, I'm coming."

After descending the other side, Spike sat in his open-air cell. It reminded him of the hole. Except this time, the diseased couldn't reach through to him.

Still no water, Spike chewed on his bread, so dry he found it almost impossible to swallow. He stared up at the slowly darkening sky. No way could he look for Matilda at night. Bad enough when he could see where he was going.

Once he'd finished eating, his skin cooling as the sweat on it dried, Spike leaned against one of the rough walls and closed his eyes. The tormented scream of the diseased rang through the darkening city like the howling of wolves.

CHAPTER 36

⁂

Spike woke to the bright sun shining down on him through the top of the wrecked building like an interrogator's spotlight. It set fire to his eyes and it took him a few seconds to get his vision back. It helped when it moved behind a grey cloud, dropping the temperature a little. Because of the angle he'd slept at, a sharp pain ran down the right side of his neck and streaked through his back. But at least he'd slept. His mouth tasted like stale bread, his tongue sticking to the roof of it as he swallowed. On top of the pain in his neck and back, every muscle in his body ached, rooting him to the spot. What was he doing here? How could he hope to find Matilda in this mess of a city? Was she even still alive? But he had to check the ruins on the hill. It would be pointless to give up before he'd been there. Also, if *he'd* managed to survive a night, then she sure as hell had.

While getting to his feet, Spike did his best to suppress his groan. Not that he'd heard anything outside the walls of the small building, but better to be safe.

The same vines Spike had used to access the building lined the walls on the inside. After strapping his bread bag around his waist and resheathing his sword, he reached up and grabbed the knotted vines. A tug to test their strength, the entire plant moved but held. He started his climb.

At the top of the wall, Spike fixed on the ruins on the hill. Matilda had to be there. When they were on the roof of the gym, she'd told him that was where she'd go. It would have taken more than a few diseased to get in her way. But why would she have gone there rather than headed back to Edin? In his haste to get to her, he'd not considered it. Surely if she had the skills to get through the city, she had the skills to get home. As he thought about it, he focused on what he felt in his heart. She was alive. He couldn't prove it, but he knew it. And even if she hadn't made it, he had to find evidence before he gave up his search.

Just before Spike climbed down, he froze. Beneath him, standing on the opposite side of the wall to where he'd slept, stood a diseased. Somehow, the thing hadn't noticed him yet.

Spike slowly drew his sword, holding his breath as if it would somehow quiet the action.

After swinging his legs over so they hung above the beast, Spike counted down from three and slipped off the wall, leading with the tip of his sword. His weight and momentum drove his blade through the top of the creature's skull. He let go of his weapon, allowing it to fall away with the monster.

The uneven ground made an unfortunate landing pad, Spike's foot turning on a rock. He slammed down against his left shoulder, fighting to contain his yell.

Deep breaths helped, and as Spike got to his feet, he tested his ankle. He could still stand. While riding his rapid pulse, he looked around, leaning down to the dead diseased to retrieve his sword from its new flesh sheath. It came free with a moist squelch.

After a few seconds of near silence, his senses on high alert, Spike nodded. No other diseased in the area, he gulped again and moved off at a quiet jog in the direction of the ruins on the hill.

CHAPTER 37

⮘⮚

For the second time in as many minutes, Spike faced the sky with his mouth open and walked into a large rock. His shin lit up with a sharp pain as he went over the top of it and landed hard. The rough ground tore fire through his palms. Everything aching, he rolled onto his back and opened his mouth like he'd been doing for the past half an hour since it had started raining. It had taken a while to quench his thirst, but he'd now drunk enough of the hot downpour to sate the dry pinch at the back of his throat.

Spike got to his feet again and looked up the hill. While green and grassy from where nature had taken the city back, now he'd gotten closer to it, he saw it sat upon a base of black rock. The ruins looked hundreds of years old. Thousands even. What would it have looked like back in the day? What had the structure been? It had clearly been built to a higher standard than the thick wall surrounding Edin. Maybe they'd had the luxury of being able to travel for supplies. Everything they built in Edin had to be scavenged by a handful of protectors, or made from what surrounded them. Most of their weapons came from scraps brought back from the ruined city. It was why they broke apart so easily.

The place certainly had metal in abundance. Spindly rods of

steel poked from every fallen structure. The ancients must have used it to strengthen their buildings so they could dominate the skyline.

Only a third of the way up the steep hill, the effort had left Spike breathless. A large open space stretched out in front of him, giving him a level surface to walk along as a moment of respite. Flagstones—cracked and defeated by nature—covered the ground of the wide plateau. The rain came down even harder as if redoubling its efforts, the heavy drops stinging as they crashed against the top of his head. The climb had been hard, but it would have been much harder in the summer sun.

When Spike had crossed the flagstones, he came to what looked like a bridge. Or rather, what used to be a bridge. Most of it remained intact, but the final ten feet was completely missing. Cracks ran through it as if it could fall at any moment. On the other side stood what looked like an entryway of some sort. At one time, it would have no doubt been much taller and had an arch over it. Now, two broken walls—standing no higher than about five feet each—remained on either side of the narrow entrance.

It looked like a statue had once stood on each side of the wall too. All that remained was their boots and the bottoms of their swords. Maybe they were their world's protectors. What battles had they fought? Had there always been diseased?

Spike walked to the edge of the remaining bridge and looked down. The sight of the forty-foot drop lifted his stomach. It ended on a bed of jagged rock. Bleached bones littered the spiky surface. Human bones. Hopefully diseased bones.

But other people had faced the dilemma of accessing the ruins, because thick metal poles had been driven into the stone bridge beneath Spike's feet, giving him a platform to walk across. Four two-inch thick bars, four inches of space between each one. They were slick with rainwater, but if he took his time, and if they held his weight, he should be able to walk across them. However, they didn't fully cross the gap. They fell short by about four feet. An easy jump in any other situation.

Before he stepped on the poles, a strong gust of wind hit Spike, flipping his stomach for the second time. He imagined his body slamming against the rocks. Another look at the bleached bones. Had the diseased died instantly when they fell, or had they lain there broken for days?

Another look at the ruins. He had to check them for Matilda. If she'd made it to the city, she'd be in there somewhere. If only he could call out to her.

Spike sat on the bridge and rested his feet against the poles, testing them to see if they'd take his weight. It felt like they would. The wet ground soaked into his trousers where he sat, and he pressed down again as another test. The poles remained strong. They must have been driven deeply into the stone bridge.

Spike's legs shook when he stood on the poles, his arms thrust out for balance. Adrenaline quickened his heart rate. The bars held.

The poles bounced with Spike's weight as he shuffled along them to the four-foot gap at the end. It reminded him of the stories they'd told him at school about pirates and being made to walk the plank. They talked about the high seas and he never knew if they were real or not. Never mind shark-infested waters, the teeth-like rocks below him would tear him to shreds.

At the edge of the poles, Spike tried to drag composure into his body with deep breaths. It did little to calm him down. He looked up at the ruins again. She had to be in there.

A silent countdown from three, Spike used the bounce in the poles before he leaped. As he pushed off, his thrust failed him when his feet slipped on the wet metal.

CHAPTER 38

The fear of the jump took the strength from Spike's legs, so when he landed on the other side, he stumbled for several steps before crashing down against the hard ground, his knees smashing against the broken rocks. He stifled his gasp as he looked for signs of the diseased.

As Spike stood up, wincing from yet more pains in his body, he continued to scan the ruins in front of him. The main site sat at the top of another hill.

Although he'd kept his noise down, Spike halted when he heard the scuffle of footsteps, the sound of a diseased coming to investigate. What had once been a stone hut of some sort on his right, he darted for it and pressed his back against the still-standing wall, hiding from the approaching creature.

His heart on overdrive, Spike fought against his panicked breaths and listened to the beast closing in on him. The awkward shuffle sounded like it dragged one of its feet. A snuffling growl combined with the phlegmy rattle in its chest. Just one of them, so maybe it hadn't heard him. It hadn't yet loosed a shriek.

As the creature drew closer, Spike unsheathed his sword.

Blood stained the blade. More blood would stain it before he returned to the city with his love.

The creature came into view, walking past Spike in the direction of the entryway he'd just fallen through. It swung its head from side to side, but it clearly couldn't see, the sticky blood clogging its eye sockets. It had once been a man. It stood shorter than Spike, but its skin looked like it might once have been as dark. The disease had turned it pale.

A twist of revulsion turned through Spike to watch it work its jaw as if it chewed on the air around it. It had a dark hole in its cheek, highlights of white puss oozing from the wound as if it sweated the foul secretion.

A widening of his stance, Spike raised his sword. Something about his movement must have alerted the creature. It spun on him, its mouth falling wide like many he'd seen before. Its chest lifted with an inhale, but before it could make a sound, Spike thrust the tip of his sword into its dark and foetid mouth. The blade sank into its face, running out of the back of its head and severing its spinal column.

Spike pulled his sword out again before the creature fell and dragged it with it. For a second, he watched the thing on the ground. He then poked his head from his hiding spot. The way looked clear. For now.

CHAPTER 39

Spike's calves ached from the climb and where he'd moved on tiptoes to keep his noise down. His eyes stung from a mixture of tiredness, the hard rain, and him blinking as little as possible so he could scan the surrounding ruins. The creatures could spring on him from anywhere. Now he'd nearly made it to the top, his heart beat faster, butterflies of anxiety tearing through his stomach. What if Matilda wasn't there?

At the top of the hill, Spike saw the extent of the ruins. They'd stood out from the gym roof, yet he'd still underestimated just how far they stretched. A space as large as the national service area, it was covered in fallen buildings, many of the walls still over eight feet tall. Where to start looking for her? When they were kids, they'd played hide-and-seek. Matilda had hidden so well no one found her. Eventually, they assumed she'd gone home and gave up. The next day, Matilda had come into school with her two front teeth missing and bruises all over her body. They were her baby teeth, so they grew back. Turned out she'd fallen asleep and had missed her dinner. Her parents were going out of their minds with worry. Her dad had a strange way of expressing his concern.

Spike had given up on her then, but he wouldn't give up on her now.

If Matilda heard Spike's voice, she'd come out. If Matilda heard Spike's voice, the countless diseased undoubtedly lurking in the ruins would also hear his voice. They'd find him quicker than she would. But what else could he do?

The rain continued to slam down, his environment glistening with damp. If he went about it silently, systematically searching the ruins, it could take him hours, and she might be on the move too, ending up somewhere he'd already looked. He had no other choice but to call for her.

A look behind at the hill he'd just scaled, Spike shook his head. Maybe he'd lost his mind. After drawing a deep breath, he yelled, "Matilda!" His voice ran away from him and soared through the ancient ruins.

When nothing responded, he tried again. "Matilda!"

A snarling hiss announced the arrival of a diseased woman. She burst from the ruins wearing jeans and a torn top, her fat sagging breasts swaying with her run.

While fixing on the creature closing down on him, Spike screamed, delivering the word as a war cry, "*Matilda!*"

The diseased responded in kind with a shrill and broken shriek. While closing down on him, her legs wobbled like they could give out beneath her. The diseased always looked one step away from a fall.

Bleach's voice came to Spike. *Hold your line and let them come to you.* The beast just a few feet away, he roared, "Matilda," and hacked his sword in a downwards diagonal slash that embedded in the side of its head. He stamped on her skull when she'd fallen. It took several attempts to break the bone. Much like when Ranger had attacked the turned Mercy.

More screams from different parts of the ruins. Another wave of creatures appeared and closed in on him. "Matilda! Matilda! Matilda!"

They came from behind every wall.

A boy—no older than about twelve when he'd turned—reached Spike next.

Spike ran the tip of his sword into the centre of the wretched thing's face. It turned limp. "Matilda!"

Too many diseased to fight, Spike tried one last time, his delivery so forceful it punched stars through his vision. "Matilda."

Hard to turn his back on the things, but he had no choice. Spike ran down the hill, the sheen on the wet ground reminding him he could slip at any moment. And from the sound behind him, some of the diseased were doing just that.

His attention on his path, Spike jumped rocks and swerved around the holes in the ground. The sound of the shrieking masses behind him grew in volume.

Spike gave over to gravity and let the hill's gradient carry him. He remained focused on what lay ahead: the small space between the two broken walls, the bars and bridge on the other side of the gap. Where the poles had looked like a makeshift walkway from the other side, they now looked like spears ready to run him through. And if they didn't, he might mistime the jump and shatter on the rocks below.

It seemed like a pointless call, but he shouted anyway as he leaped. "Matilda!"

The hill had given Spike the momentum to clear both the four-foot gap and the poles. When he hit the stone ground on the other side, his legs gave way, throwing him into a sideways roll. Fire ran through his right shoulder from taking the brunt of the impact.

Spike jumped to his feet, sword still in hand, and ran back to the edge of the broken bridge. For the first time since turning his back on them, he saw just how many diseased were chasing him. Close to one hundred of the vile things, they rushed at him, falling down the gap he'd just crossed, like stampeding cattle driven from a cliff. So preoccupied with getting to him, they didn't even seem to notice the drop.

Many heads made the poles ring like bells as they tripped and clattered into them. One beast even made the jump before it slipped on one of the poles and fell.

A bar similar to the ones drilled into the stone lay on the ground near Spike. About two feet in length, it served as the perfect club. After he'd sheathed his sword, Spike picked it up, waited for the next creature to travel too close, and cracked it in the face with a hard swing.

The bodies mounted up on the ground, and Spike continued to shout Matilda's name as he smashed the few that got too near. The rain came down hard, he sweated beneath his clothes, and his throat hurt from shouting, but his adrenaline banished any hint of fatigue.

◊

Spike didn't know how long had passed. Long enough for the rocks below to be littered with the fallen. Every one of them appeared broken in some way, and if they weren't, the sheer distance between him and them rendered their threat null and void. When he'd been chased, it looked like over one hundred of the things followed him. Now he had an aerial view of the carnage, he saw it to be even more than that.

As Spike's adrenaline rush eased, he looked back up the hill at the ruins. His search for Matilda had only just begun. Like he'd done before, he edged out onto the poles. This time, the ends of them were covered with the blood and flesh of the fallen diseased.

One more look at the writhing and broken bodies below, he spat into the hellish pit before jumping the gap back through the entryway and setting off up the hill for a second time in search of his love.

CHAPTER 40

Out of breath from climbing the hill for a second time, small spasms ran through Spike's strained calves as he took a moment to fill his lungs and look at the sprawling ruins. His knuckles ached from his grip on his broadsword. He called her name again. "Matilda!" The word took flight and then died in what remained of the old grand building. Not even a sound wave fancied the search.

The rain had eased to a fine haze that forced Spike into a permanent squint. While scanning the ruins for more emerging diseased, he tried again. "Matilda!"

Nothing else for it, Spike walked towards the wreck of a building, stepped on a fallen part of what had once been a wall, and entered the ruins of the old structure. If Edin ever fell, the buildings in it and the surrounding wall would come apart in years rather than centuries. But they had to make do with what they had. Supplies were short; mud, water, dry grass, and stones weren't.

Now inside the building, Spike took a turn through what must have once been an entrance. He found himself in a corridor and looked both left and right. The long walkway stretched off an almost equal distance in each direction. "Matilda!" His voice ricocheted off the walls.

The sound started quietly in the distance, the slightest slap of feet against stone. An uneven gallop, Spike heard the heavy rattle of diseased respiration riding along with it, almost as if the laboured pants gave the creature locomotion. The sound came from his left, so he shrugged. "Left it is, then."

Spike moved at a tiptoed jog towards the creature, his sword pointing out in front of him, his frame dropped slightly lower to give him more of a base to—the thing appeared sooner than he'd expected. He drove his sword into its chest and a spray of blood came back at him. The creature yelled. A woman with long greasy black hair and bloody eyes, she stared at him, her mouth spread wide.

While clenching his jaw, Spike kicked the thing off his sword before bringing his heavy blade down on top of its head. Another spray of warm blood ran up his front, and the creature fell against the wall. Limp. Dead.

After wiping the blood from his face, Spike rounded the corner and walked in the direction the diseased had come from. Better to be predator than prey.

~

A DEEP THROBBING ACHE IN SPIKE'S LEGS REMINDED HIM HE'D not had enough rest. The climb up the hill twice, running from the diseased, moving on tiptoes before he'd decided to shout so he didn't need to keep his noise down anymore. So far, he'd only met diseased on top of diseased on top of diseased. At least they had the good grace to seek him out in ones and twos. In the tight corridors, he didn't know how he'd cope with a horde.

The rain had now stopped, the sun pushing through what had been a sky filled with thick clouds. His top rigid from where the blood of the diseased had dried, he also wore a crusty layer on his skin. Although, no matter how bloody anyone got fighting the good fight, it didn't have the same contagious effect as saliva. As long as they didn't spit in his mouth or bite him, he'd be fine.

The next diseased to round the corner stood no more than four feet tall. The child must have been younger than ten when they were turned. A few weeks ago a pang of remorse might have twisted through Spike at the passing of such a young soul; now he just saw the enemy in its vicious crimson glare. An enemy that stood between him and Matilda.

Like he'd done with all the others, Spike let the creature come to him. He wound his sword back, the corridor wider than most, and swung for the kid when it got near. His blow landed true, liberating the tiny demon of its small head. The skinny and withered body fell forward.

The child's bloody glare stood in stark contrast to its pasty skin. Although severed from its body, it fixed on Spike, its mouth snapping.

While sneering at the vile thing, Spike lifted his leg before stamping down on its head. He crushed it in one. Compared to an adult's skull, it gave like a chicken's egg.

The same and only word he'd cried since he'd been on top of the hill, Spike stared down at the pitiful thing, letting out the confusion in his heart at taking someone so young. "Matilda!" It didn't matter how much he tried to see them as monsters, they were just kids.

∽

LIKE A GHOST WANDERING THE HALLS, SEARCHING FOR PEOPLE from a different time and a different life, Spike trudged through the ruins. Sweating in the now scorching day, every time he wiped his brow, his hand came back covered in the blood of the slain. "Matilda!" He sounded like a madman, cursed for all time as he wailed for his love. Yet he continued to yell as if cursing the gods. "Matilda."

It felt like days had passed, but the sun still shone bright, beating down on him as he scoured the place. Maybe two hours had gone by, maybe as many as four.

~

THE THOUGHT HAD BEEN CHIPPING AWAY AT HIM, GOADING HIM every time he said her name.

"Matilda!"

Give up.

"Matilda!"

She's dead.

"Matilda!"

And now you can't help Artan either.

But he continued to call her name, his throat sore, which turned his voice hoarse.

Spike had no idea where he was until he turned through another entrance and found himself back where he'd started. Two diseased walked amongst the rocks and fallen walls. They were yet to see him. Two men, both of them about his size. One of them had no clothes on his bottom half other than a pair of brown leather boots and torn socks. The tongues of the boots lolled like that of a parched dog. Its pathetic penis had nowhere near as much glory. The other wore a suit of some sort, the front torn open, a large circular wound—ridged with teeth marks—on its abdomen.

When Spike cleared his throat, two faces turned his way. Two pairs of bleeding eyes. Two open and snarling mouths. They charged, and he did what he'd done for the past several hours. He made sure his feet were planted, he wound his sword back, and he let them come to him.

∽

Nowhere near evening, but if Spike wanted to get back into Edin, he'd have to leave soon to make sure he caught the protectors on their return. They wouldn't let him back in if he rocked up on his own—not without someone vouching for him. There seemed little point in spending another night in the devastated city. She'd gone. The sooner he accepted that and faced his fate, the better.

Although he didn't have the same motivation he'd had on the first time around, Spike sheathed his sword and ran through the entryway towards the gap in the bridge. The second he leapt, the smell of the diseased hit him. An acrid vinegar tang mixed with sweat and excrement. Several hours in the sun had turned them positively toxic.

Where Spike had cleared the gap the last time, this time he landed on the metal poles, turning his feet sideways to give him the best chance of not slipping. But the pole he put most of his weight on gave beneath him. His stomach rushed into his throat as the metal bar pushed up through its stone casing. The pit of broken and still-writhing diseased below, he dropped towards them fast.

Just before he fell past them, Spike grabbed another one of the poles with both hands. One hand slipped while the other held. He hung there for a few seconds, looking at the bodies below. The rocks would shatter many things, but now the diseased covered them, they'd cushion his fall. Many limbs still moved, the jaws of half-dead creatures opened and closed as if they sensed they could make one more kill before they passed, and some of the monsters still groaned. Even the most active were broken beyond healing, but not so broken that they couldn't commit the final act of sinking their teeth into his soft flesh.

Spike managed to reach up with his loose hand and grip another one of the three remaining poles. As he hung there, exhausted both mentally and physically, his shoulders on fire with having to maintain his current position, he looked down again. Swinging because of the momentum of his fall, he watched the hellish orgy of broken bodies and muttered the only word he had left in him. "Matilda, Matilda, Matilda."

A slight loosening of his grip. Many pairs of wide and bleeding eyes looked up at him. With Matilda gone, his chances of saving Artan ruined, and the thought of facing Ranger when he got back to the national service area, Spike let out a deep sigh, muttered, "Matilda," and loosened his grip a little more.

CHAPTER 41

Spike didn't know where he'd found the will to pull himself up from the poles. Maybe stubbornness. After all this time, he couldn't let the diseased take him. So tired, he fell into every step as he stumbled through the ruined city, but he had to keep going. On more than one occasion, he tilted sideways, his legs just about ready to give up. Not enough food and nowhere near enough water, his throat had swollen, making every gulp feel like he swallowed glass. A rock of nausea balled in his gut. While he walked, he fished a chunk of bread from his bag and chewed on it. It sated his hunger but heightened his thirst, his eyes watering every time he swallowed.

Although he knew his way back, what would he do when he returned to Edin? He still had a few weeks of national service ahead. A few weeks of being reminded he'd lost both his love and his chance at freedom. Were it not for Artan, he wouldn't be going back at all. But there had to be a way to free him like he'd promised. There had to be.

Spike hung his head as he walked. In his mind, he heard the berating he'd get from Sarge and Bleach. He listened to Ranger's snark and saw the stares from many of the other cadets, even if they didn't say anything. They wouldn't need to. But he owed this to Matilda. To her memory.

Despite the total destruction everywhere he looked, Spike had made a map in his mind based on landmarks. Degraded and devastated by nature, he still recognised the tall tower he'd seen on his way in. Taller than any other structure in the surrounding area, it had a rusty metal skeleton that still pointed to the sky, lasting longer than the grey rock that clung to it. It looked ready to fall at any moment, yet it still remained defiant against entropy.

A sinkhole had claimed half the road from where it had taken a bite from the city. Rubble filled a lot of it, but it still stood out enough for Spike to recognise.

Close to exiting the city, gulping repeatedly as if it would somehow help his throat, Spike suddenly heard voices and froze. He crouched down behind a large rock, his legs sore with fatigue.

A trio of protectors, they walked in size order. Hulk, as the team leader, led them. The large dark-skinned man had both his swords drawn, ready to end any diseased that dared come close. He had two trainees with him.

Hopefully they hadn't seen him, and thank god they didn't have Magma in their party. Were he to run into the leader of the protectors out there on his own, the man would probably slit his throat and leave him for dead. After what had gone on with Spike and Ranger, Spike wouldn't blame him if he did. But because they didn't have Magma, there seemed little point in hiding. The sun had gotten lower in the sky, so they had to be heading back. He stood up.

But before any of the protectors noticed him, something caught Spike's eye. The glint of something metal on the ground. Hard to tell, but it looked like Matilda's hummingbird clip. His mum's hummingbird clip.

Spike dropped down again, his breaths running quicker than

before. He listened to the voices of the protectors as they moved through the ruins, chatting like they hadn't noticed him.

Once the voices had walked away, Spike poked his head up over the rock and gasped.

Greeted by the demonic leer of Hulk, Spike jumped to his feet and backed away.

"Well, well, if it isn't our escapee."

The two trainees had clearly walked on to make him reveal himself.

"We thought you'd be dead by now." Hulk laughed and shook his head while looking Spike up and down. "Although from the state of you, I'm guessing you've seen your fair share of action. You been bitten?"

Spike watched the protector.

"What's wrong? Diseased got your tongue?"

"What do you want?"

"To take you back. To rescue you."

Spike took another step away from him. "And what if I don't need rescuing?"

"If you're out here, you *need* rescuing."

From the way the protectors tensed as he took another step back, Spike could tell they had their orders. If they found him, they had to bring him back. They weren't offering him a choice.

Spike filled his lungs and shouted through the pain in his throat, "Matilda!"

All three protectors stared at him. One of the trainees tilted her head to the side. "What are you doing?"

"Matilda! Matilda! Matilda!"

Hulk pointed both swords at Spike. "If I have to silence you, boy, I will."

"Matilda!"

Before Hulk could say anything else, the screaming diseased responded to Spike's call. He'd never been more pleased to hear them. The three protectors had a Pavlovian response to the sound, raising their weapons and spinning to face their aggressors.

Spike didn't need any more of an invitation. He set off in the opposite direction, Hulk calling after him, "You fool. You're going to die out here."

The sound of his own breaths running through his head, his legs weak as he weaved through the derelict city, Spike pushed on. Maybe he would regret it, but not as much as he'd regret leaving the hummingbird clip. He had to follow the trail to the end. He'd thought it since she'd gone missing and it now felt stronger than ever. Matilda was alive. If anyone could survive out here, she could. Now he just needed to find her.

CHAPTER 42

A few hours had passed before Spike returned to the spot of his encounter with the protectors. The bodies of at least ten diseased lay on the ground. Beheaded, stabbed through the face, and stomped to death. It looked like the protectors had made light work of them.

When Spike saw a flask left on the rock he'd hidden behind, he looked around for the three protectors. He couldn't see them. He walked towards it like an animal being lured into a trap.

Spike picked up the flask, the container heavy with liquid. While loosening the lid, he continued to watch his surroundings. Still no sign of the protectors, he drank the water, draining the container in several desperate gulps.

Although Spike's thirst remained, albeit much lessened for the drink, his slightly moistened mouth allowed him to eat more bread. While he chewed on a chunk, he walked over to the hummingbird clip, the world turning orange in the setting sun. The ruins stretched away from him, the clip giving him no more than an indication of where Matilda might have gone. Too late to look for her now, he needed rest and daylight.

A large metal sheet at least an inch thick and six feet square lay on the ground. It was close to a pit it looked like it had once covered. A hiding place lost to time. Maybe he'd find somewhere better if he searched, but after his trip to the hole, a night in a pit would feel like a luxury.

Although he hadn't heard any, Spike glanced around to look for diseased before he slipped into the shallow grave and dragged the heavy sheet over the top of him. As much as he wanted to find Matilda, it would be suicide to do it at night and with how tired he felt. Tomorrow was a new day. Tomorrow he'd be reunited with his love.

CHAPTER 43

The rattling sound of thunder woke Spike, his heart damn near exploding from the violent interruption to his sleep. His saliva had turned into a funky paste, and fur covered his teeth, which his sandpaper tongue could do nothing to remove. A paranoia he woke with many mornings struck him: how many bugs had crawled down his throat in the night? His fear worse than usual because the dark pit had to be crawling with them.

Then Spike heard the sound again. The darkness rendered him blind, but he blinked repeatedly until he saw small slivers of daylight around the edge of the metal sheet. Another rumble above. Except, now he'd regained his lucidity, his heart kicked, forcing a gasp from him. Not thunder. He listened to it again: the awkward gait of a diseased above.

Fumbling around in the gritty darkness, Spike first found his bag of sweaty and broken bread before he found his sheathed sword. A shudder writhed through him. He must have shared his bed with hundreds of creatures. Millipedes, woodlice, beetles … he shuddered again. But he'd have to stay in the insect world's playground for a while longer. He hugged his sword to his chest. He needed to wait for the diseased to move on.

∼

Maybe five minutes, maybe more, the daylight taunted Spike. A commodity he couldn't afford to squander. Not if he wanted to find Matilda today. But the diseased hadn't moved on. It sounded like only one of them, but the thing continued its back and forth on the sheet above.

As thunder ran over him again—the edges of the sheet rattling against the stone ground—Spike shivered from an excess of adrenaline. The need to take action twitched through him. The creature sounded different to many he'd heard before. Still the shrill calls and phlegmy rattle he'd grown used to, but this one had a slightly different pitch to it. Almost like it was enjoying itself.

Not only was Spike wasting time by remaining in the self-made coffin, but the more noise the diseased made, the higher the risk it would attract others.

Nothing else for it, Spike kept his sword in one hand and reached up with the other, feeling the cold and rough underside of the steel sheet. He pushed against it, but it didn't budge.

A hard clench to his jaw, he pushed again. Nothing.

When he pushed for a third time, grunting with the effort, the diseased creature made it even harder for him, its clumsy steps shifting so it stood directly above.

After putting his sword down, Spike tried again. Not even two hands were enough to shift it.

The effort left Spike out of breath, the confined space amplifying his struggle. The diseased grew louder, its steps sounding like the thing skipped in circles. The more pleasure it got from the sound, the longer it would stay. The longer it stayed, the more noise it would make, and the higher the risk of it attracting friends. He needed a way out now. If he didn't find one, he'd perish in a grave of his own making.

∽

Billy Groves from textiles had fallen into what had initially been planned as a basement in one of the factories. Before Spike and Matilda's time, but all the kids talked about it. He'd been exploring the building site and had fallen into the deep hole. He could have climbed out, but when the hatch fell closed, he didn't have the strength to push it open again. They said he was eight years old at the time and the large wooden door would have been a struggle for a fully grown man. Since that day, they made sure every hatch had double doors so even a child could move them.

As kids, they'd often walk past the warehouse he'd died in. Sometimes they'd sneak a look through the window at the large wooden doors covering the basement. Billy had fallen in at a time when the building work had been put on hold because of a lack of supplies. Over a week had passed before they found his corpse.

Spike and Matilda had talked about what they'd do if they were trapped. They imagined Billy made a lot of noise, but no one heard him, the thick wood muffling the boy's cries. Matilda said she'd find some flint and set fire to it. Wood burns, but wood that thick would take more than a spark to set it ablaze. And how would she find flint in a dark basement?

Despite years of deliberation, they never came up with an idea on what to do. They imagined Billy screaming until he lost his voice. His hands were broken, so he must have attacked the barrier to no avail.

But Spike wasn't Billy, and Spike wasn't a child. The restrictions nature placed on the poor little boy didn't apply to him. The one thing he could take from Billy's case was waiting it out wouldn't work.

Before Spike could formulate a plan, the sound of another

diseased's steps hit the steel sheet. Two of them beat an uneven tattoo above. "Dammit," Spike muttered. "Dammit."

∼

THE SECOND DISEASED SHOWED SPIKE THEY'D KEEP COMING IF HE didn't do something. A dumb and obvious plan, but the only one he had, Spike raised the hilt of his sword as another line of thunder ripped over his head, and he slammed it against the metal ceiling.

The thunder stopped. At least two creatures, they both froze. Were they capable of it, he was sure they would have spoken to one another. Instead, he imagined them staring into each other's bleeding eyes, what little processing power they had left in their brains working overtime to understand the noise. However, despite their reaction, they hadn't yet moved—at least it didn't sound like they had. When he pushed against the sheet above him, it remained as impossible to lift.

How many ways had Billy Groves tried to get himself free? "Get off!" Spike shouted, kicking against the sheet. "Get the hell off." He banged and punched up at the metal, the hard barrier stinging his knuckles. "Get off! Get off! Get off!"

The sound above him changed. Where he'd heard what he believed to be an approximation of joy from the beasts, he now heard the familiar shrill call of a predator. They weren't playing anymore. But they moved away, and this time, when he pushed against the sheet, it lifted … until thunder ran over it again and it slammed down.

"Warghhh!" Spike yelled and kicked up, the sheet ringing like an industrial bell. "Get the hell off, now." For a second time, he listened to the creatures step away. The noise must have freaked them out.

A deep breath, Spike moved in one fluid motion. He lifted the sheet, hooked his grip over the edge of it, and shoved it away from him. The sound of steel screeched over the stone ground before the weight of the creatures jumped on it again, slamming it down so it closed the lid. Although now he had a bar of daylight about an inch thick.

Spike's heart damn near burst when a pair of diseased eyes appeared in the gap. Then the other pair. The small coffin filled with the vinegar reek of decay, the funk of putridity forced in on their heavy and hot breaths. Still just two, they seemed more concerned with getting at him than alerting others.

The shallow grave made the angle awkward, but Spike managed to shift his broadsword so he could point it through the gap. Not much space to drive it up with, but enough. He clenched his jaw and shoved the tip of his blade into the first eye. It sank with a wet squelch.

Like a split bladder, the eye leaked blood in a water-falling rush. Although Spike turned his face away from it, the warm splash hit his neck and cheek. The smell thickened to the point where he gagged on the air, several heaves lifting a bitter-tasting bile onto the back of his tongue. Doing the same with the second creature, he stuck it and then dodged another wash of blood as the thing collapsed where it stood, a heavy thud against the metal sheet.

Other than the sound of his own breath, Spike heard nothing. Just two and he'd gotten them both. Their faces still leaked blood into the hole. Spike put his sword down and reached up for the now slippery edge of the sheet. While grunting from the effort, he shifted the sheet down, pushing towards his toes so the gap grew. Despite the weight of the bodies, he managed to slide it where he hadn't been able to lift.

When Spike had dragged the gap wide enough, the first diseased fell on top of him. A moment later, the dead weight of the second one spilled in. Like with the splash back, he turned his face away from their bleeding bodies, the two corpses joining him in his grave. But he'd done it. The metal sheet now free, his sword back in his hand, he reached down for his bag of bread but found it in a pool of their blood, soaking up the diseased fluid. "Dammit."

His hands soaked, his clothes soaked, his arms sore with the effort, Spike blinked against the bright summer sun. He sat up in his grave and wiped some of the diseased blood from his face and neck. Then he saw them … Magma, Warrior, and one of his trainees. They had a pile of diseased bodies around them, their freshly spilled rancid blood shimmering in the bright sun.

Jezebel in hand, a claret goo dripping from both sides, Magma's face showed Spike where Ranger had gotten it from. A sadistic leer, he snorted an ironic laugh. "Well, well, well. Looks like we've caught our fish. And good job we were here. Two diseased is manageable, but the other eight would have ruined you. Come on, boy, you've had your fun; now it's time to go home."

CHAPTER 44

It might have been a night in a self-imposed grave, but Spike felt energised because of the rest. Under the scrutiny of Magma, Warrior, and the trainee, he burst from the pit. Closer to his destination than they were, he sprinted in the direction he believed Matilda had gone.

Magma's order chased on his heels. "Wait there! Come back."

Let them try to catch him. All three of them were too big and too slow. No way would they get him back to Edin, not now he had a lead on Matilda.

Although Spike didn't look around as he weaved through the fallen rocks, he didn't need to, the clumsy steps of the three protectors telling him exactly how far behind they were. None of them were as fast as him, their bodies better suited for battle.

When Spike headed for the ruins on the hill, he'd had the time to note the landmarks on his way so he could plot his return journey. He didn't have that luxury now. But then he saw he didn't need it. It might have been invisible to an untrained eye, but for him, the markings stood out from a mile away. Many of the buildings were covered in scratches and scrapes, most of the markings meaningless. However, nestled among the hatchings of ruin, he saw a heart carved into one of the walls. Matilda had traced it on him enough times for him to know exactly what he was looking at.

The sign sent a renewed vigour rushing through Spike, his legs regaining their full strength as he quickened his pace. The first heart led him through a gap between two fallen towers.

Around the next bend, the loose stones slipping beneath his feet, Spike entered what had once been a plaza. The guards continued to give chase, but their steps had grown quieter from where he'd already opened a lead.

There were no signs in the immediate vicinity, so Spike ran across the square. Six possible routes, he looked at each of them as Magma's voice behind him commanded, "Stay there, boy."

Spike spun around to see the protectors hadn't yet made it into the plaza.

Then Warrior appeared, red-faced and moving quicker than the other two. "Don't be a fool. Come back to Edin with us."

Too exposed in the square, Spike took the next path on his left. Dread sank through him the second he entered it. No time to turn around, he ran at the dead end. The wall stood at least thirty feet tall. The grey stone and brick looked impassable. The walls along either side, although not as imposing, were still too high to climb. The alley spread too wide to kick from one to the other like he and Matilda had done when they'd run from Edin's guards.

Now committed, Spike dashed to the end, the steps of the protectors reminding him they weren't slowing down. At least if he had his back to the wall, he could fight them from there. No way were they taking him in. Not now he had further evidence of Matilda being alive.

At the dead end, the protectors close to entering the alley, Spike saw something and his heart lifted. A crack ran down each side of the tall wall. The gap looked large enough for him to slip his boyish frame through. Just. Which meant the protectors had no chance.

While staring back up the alley in the direction of the plaza, Spike pushed his arm through the gap up to his shoulder. Although the rough walls scraped, tearing burning cuts into his front and back, he managed to force his chest through. He turned his head sideways, keeping his attention focused on where he expected the protectors to appear. One final push, he held his breath, bit down against the stinging cuts, and shoved himself the rest of the way through.

On the other side Spike gasped and took several calming breaths, sweat burning the scrapes on his body. Trapped and then free again in the space of a few seconds, he found himself in what would have once been a ground-floor room, but the wreckage in his way stood even taller than the dead-end wall. Rubble blocked what used to be a doorway out of there. He had to hide and wait for the protectors to give up so he could exit the small space the same way he'd entered.

Warrior ran into the alleyway first, his slightly erratic tone bouncing off the tight walls as he fought to catch his breath. "Where's he gone? The little brat. I tell you this for nothing, I don't want to spend my day chasing an ungrateful little shit around this city."

No reply from the other two. Although he couldn't see him, Spike imagined Magma scanning his environment, looking from side to side, sniffing the air like a wolf on a fox's scent. He'd flush him out in a heartbeat.

While scanning the small space for somewhere better to hide, Spike looked up. He should have noticed it sooner. Where the crack ran down both sides of the dead-end wall, severing it from the buildings on either side, it had compromised its structure. Thirty feet of brick and stone swayed like a drunkard. No doubt he'd made it worse when he squeezed through the gap.

The steps of the three protectors came towards the wall, and although Spike didn't want to be caught by them, he didn't want them to be crushed either. He couldn't return to Edin if they died while trying to bring him back.

Magma's deep voice went off like a fired cannon. "I think we should cut our losses and move on. God knows where he's gone, but like Warrior, I don't want to spend my day searching for him."

Despite his words, their footsteps continued towards Spike. He watched the top of the swaying wall. If he warned the protectors, he'd blow his cover. And now he'd seen the heart, there was no way he'd be going back to Edin before he found Matilda.

Debris crunched beneath the protectors' heavy steps. They were just feet away. But then they stopped. A shrill call in the square. Spike heard the quick shuffle of feet from where they turned to face the noise.

"Come on," Warrior said. "Let's do what we came here to do. The boy will turn up."

While listening to Warrior run off, Spike watched the hypnotic sway of the wall.

As the sound of more diseased closed in on the protectors, the trainee said, "I'll go and help Warrior."

But even though her feet ran away from him, Magma hadn't left. So close now, he only had to look through the gap and he'd see him. The man hated him, and now he had him all alone.

Spike had to tell him to get back. He'd find a way to get to Matilda, but first he had to save the protector.

CHAPTER 45

The screams in the plaza grew louder, either drowning out Magma's movement just a few feet away on the other side of the wall, or halting him completely. Spike couldn't tell. While watching the gap where he expected the protector's face to appear, his heart in his throat, Spike rode his giddy breaths and waited. Maybe Magma had seen the gap and he knew. Maybe he hadn't. Either way, could he really ignore the call to aid the others?

Magma answered his question a moment or two later, the heavy steps of the stocky brute turning around and running towards the square.

While letting go of his breath, Spike leaned against the tall wall. The second he realised his error, he looked at the top of the towering stone and brick barrier. It swayed like the long grass in the meadow, but it didn't fall. Hopefully the protectors had given up on him. Sooner or later, the wall would come crashing down, and hopefully both he and the protectors would be long gone by then.

Spike waited for at least half an hour, the sun beating down, the humidity clinging to him. The wall held, and the protectors had finished fighting in the square some time ago. He caught his breath to make his body as skinny as possible and slipped back out through the gap, his eyes on the top of the wall in case he needed to outrun it.

On the other side, Spike looked up again. The wall didn't have long left. Like many parts of this city, entropy had it in a stranglehold as it slowly choked it out. There would only be one winner. Sooner or later, the city would be no more than dust.

Back out in the square, Spike came across five headless bodies, atrophied, pale, and wrinkled like they'd spent hours submerged in water. But he didn't have time to admire the protectors' handiwork. Instead, he looked around the square. Now he didn't have the protectors on his tail, he saw it almost immediately. Another heart.

Spike followed its direction into a narrow pathway, the ground covered in fallen debris. The remaining walls pressed in from either side as if funnelling him towards something. Hopefully his love.

A small heart this time, no larger than the span of his hand, Spike took its direction and turned left.

Almost impossible to see where the path led because of the devastation, Spike somehow found a route, jumping bricks and low walls, and avoiding the sharp, strong, and rusty metal fingers protruding from the rocks. The sound of his own steps echoed in the closed space. He did his best to listen for the noises of the protectors and the diseased. He heard neither.

The heat and humidity of the day sapped Spike's strength, so he slowed to a fast walk. The tight alleyway went uphill, the strain of it taking its toll on his still sore calves. But he continued to climb, pushing through the burn as he searched the walls for another heart. He reached down to his pocket and felt the hummingbird hair clip. It helped shove his tiredness aside.

When he crested the top of the hill, Spike gasped. The word left him as a breath. "Tilly."

She stood on top of a broken plinth. Of course she'd found somewhere high and inaccessible, she was the best climber he knew. He shook his head, smiled to himself, and continued forward.

When the space opened up, Spike damn near lost his stomach. He fell two steps to the left against a small wall. Now he saw why she'd climbed the pillar.

Quieter than he'd ever seen them, they were gathered around the bottom of the plinth like worshipers at the foot of their messiah. They all fixed on her. Bleeding eyes, slack jaws, swaying bodies. One hundred diseased at least, all of them waited patiently for her to fall.

CHAPTER 46

Spike had retreated into the shadow of a nearby doorway, occasionally poking his head from it to look at his love. If anyone deserved a plinth in the middle of the city, she did. Her greatness should be elevated above the masses—just not masses of diseased.

An hour had passed, maybe more. The temperature had risen, the humidity growing thicker almost as if the gods turned up the pressure with every second of Spike's inaction. At some point he'd have to commit to his plan. Over the past ten minutes or so, he'd intended to step from the shadows several times, but his jelly legs were yet to get the message.

It made sense to wait because the protectors who'd chased him earlier needed to be well and truly away from the area. Like with the toppling wall, he didn't want to catch them in the crossfire. But enough time had passed. His reluctance now had its roots in fear.

"Come on, Spike," he muttered to himself as if hearing the words would help, "you've got to do something."

After gulping against the thick paste in his dry mouth, his throat parched, his breaths heavier because of his dehydration,

Spike stepped from the shadows again and stood at the top of the hill, looking across at the girl he loved. Tiredness dragged on her features, her eyes encircled with dark rings. If he felt thirsty having drunk something last night, how did she feel?

His hands cupped around his mouth, Spike inhaled deeply to call her name, but the shrill cry of the diseased cut him dead. They were behind him. Matilda looked over at him, and for the briefest of moments time stopped as they stared at one another. The brown eyes and beautiful face he thought he'd never see again.

Were it not for the second cry, Spike would have remained in their path. He pulled back into the shadows, his love's face twisted with confusion.

A second or two later, the diseased tore past. They were just feet from the dark doorway. They dragged their rich vinegar tang with them. They had just one purpose: get to the lady on the pillar.

If Spike waited any longer, more diseased would come. A world full of the things, time only made it worse. Although, when he stepped out again and watched the newest arrivals join the masses below, worse seemed like a clumsy thought. A word didn't exist for something beyond Matilda's current predicament.

Unlike last time, Matilda watched Spike from the start. His pulse running away with him, he looked at the creatures gathered at her feet. All of them angled their faces up. Whether they could see through their bleeding eyes or not, he didn't know. But however they did it, they knew where she stood. They sensed her and they were ready.

Spike cupped his mouth for a second time and shouted through the swollen pain of his throat. "Matilda!"

Her jaw fell slack and she turned instantly pale. Over two hundred bleeding eyes fixed on him, and a furious hiss filled the air. The hisses turned into cries, and as one, they ran at Spike.

His legs shaking, Spike sweated in the muggy heat. Despite his need to run, he had to get his words out. "Meet me at the front of this city."

But Matilda didn't respond.

In their rush to get to him, the creatures fell over the debris and one another. The leader no more than one hundred feet away, they came forward like a plague.

The ground shook as they drew closer. Spike shouted it again. "Meet me at the front of this city. Do you hear me?"

Although she nodded furiously, Matilda's face buckled with her tears.

Several of the front runners had opened up a lead. The press of so many bodies behind created a bottleneck in the narrow pathways. A glance at their furious faces, Spike's stomach clamped like he might vomit. After giving Matilda a thumbs up, he waited for the creatures at the front to get no more than about twenty feet away before he took off, leading the beasts from his love and back into the ruined city.

CHAPTER 47

The only play he had, hopefully Spike hadn't just turned his back on his love for the final time. She'd been so close to him and he'd chosen to run in the opposite direction.

The stampede behind him, Spike retraced his steps, the tighter alleys slowing down the mob on his tail. It sounded like many fell. He might have been outnumbered, but at least he had coordination on his side.

When he burst back into the plaza with the slain diseased left by Magma, Warrior, and his trainee, he ran for his intended target: the same dead-end alleyway he'd been in earlier.

The first of the diseased swarm entered the square behind him as Spike shot into the alley and charged at the dead end.

Spike shoved through the gap, faster than he had the first time, the walls tearing cuts into him that lit his sweating body with an electric buzz.

As he pushed through, Spike tripped and landed on the hard ground bottom first. The jolt sent a spasm up his back, but he didn't have time to tend to it. While sitting there, he panted and watched the gap. A few seconds later, withered arms reached in after him.

No time to rest, Spike got to his feet and drew his broadsword, his throat so dry every gulp made him heave. He swung for an intrusive arm, taking it off at the elbow. The withered appendage spasmed on the ground with an arachnid twitch.

The swell of footsteps filled the alleyway, and the arms withdrew from Spike's attack. He took to poking his sword through the gap. Every time he felt the resistance of the tip passing through shrivelled flesh, he heard a diseased's cry.

Unable to see, Spike had to rely on his ears. It sounded like the diseased had already filled the alley. Long enough to fit the entire mob, he looked at the top of the tall wall. Did it have enough stone and brick in it to crush them all? Only one way to find out.

After sheathing his sword, he shoved the wall and watched it lean away from him.

But it didn't topple.

He shoved it again, the top swaying but not falling.

The rich funk of sour vinegar and sweat grew worse because of the tight press of bodies just inches away from him. More arms reached through, a line of them from the ground to about eight feet in the air. They were climbing on top of one another to get to him. If he didn't watch out, they'd push the wall his way.

While yelling, Spike ran his sword down the forearms, dragging a cut from top to bottom. The hissing screams called rage at him. They'd get him and they knew it. It was just a matter of time.

Nothing else for it, Spike sheathed his sword again and turned to the wall behind him. A craggy face where the once building had fallen apart, it had jutting steps of stone, bricks, and metal rods giving him a path to ascend.

Spike began his climb out of what had now turned into his prison. At about forty feet, the back wall stood a good ten feet taller than the wobbly dead end he hoped to send crashing down on the diseased freaks.

∼

THE HIGHER SPIKE CLIMBED, THE MORE HIS BODY BETRAYED HIM. A sinking feeling plummeted through his stomach every time he looked down, and his legs trembled. His hands were clammy with sweat, the dust and grit clinging to them, and his eyes burned because he couldn't rub them.

When Spike reached the top, he peered over the back edge. So high, he had a view of the entire city. He looked at the plinth Matilda had been on and saw she'd gone. He looked at the ruins on the hill. The skeletal tower he thought to be the tallest building around until he saw it from his current vantage point. But when he looked down the other side for an escape route, he only saw a sheer drop.

The vines covering the wall weren't thick enough to hold Spike's weight. As one of the few walls in the city to remain intact, it ran a flush line all the way to the hard ground over forty feet below.

While blowing his cheeks out, Spike looked back at the alleyway. In his current position, he saw the tight space was packed with diseased. Then he saw what stopped the wall from falling. The same metal rods that poked from rocks all over the city tied the swaying dead end to the structure next to it. When the wall leaned forward, the resistance of the tether prevented it from toppling.

A small ledge on Spike's left led to the top of the dead-end wall and the metal tether. Despite trying to centre himself, it did nothing for his rapid pulse and shaking legs. Because he didn't have all day, he slowly shifted out across it. If he ever needed Matilda and her skills … Not only did she climb like a monkey, but she had the confidence of one too. She'd have walked the ledge as if she were no more than a few inches from the ground. But he didn't have her. And he was thirty feet up. No matter what she would have done, he needed to find his own way.

Spike moved slowly across the ledge, shuffling an inch and then stopping, testing his next step before committing to it. Several times, a chunk of rock or brick gave way, falling into the room he'd occupied when first squeezing through the gap.

It took a good few minutes to cross a space no wider than six feet, Spike's knuckles aching because of how tightly he gripped on. But he made it. In spite of the noise from the creatures below, he heard the creaking of the metal tie now he'd gotten closer.

While holding on, Spike stretched out his right leg and shoved the top of the wall. It moved with more force than before, but still halted because of the metal rod. The only way to knock the wall down would be to wrench the bar free.

So preoccupied with the metal tether, Spike stepped closer without checking. The ledge gave beneath him.

CHAPTER 48

Spike reached out as he fell and caught a metal bar poking from the wall beside him. His stomach churned to look at the drop, his legs hanging down. But he held on.

Several scrambling seconds later, Spike found a surer footing. He should have checked the first time.

Close to a panic attack, his chest heaving, Spike reached out to where the metal tether sat embedded in the solid wall and wriggled it.

At first, the rod barely moved, brick and stone dust taking flight on the gentle breeze. A tight clench to his jaw, Spike wriggled the rod harder, grunting from the effort. He'd done the tricky bit: he'd led the diseased away, he'd climbed this high, he'd helped Matilda escape; now he just needed to …

The metal rod came free. For a moment, nothing happened. And then the wall fell.

As the large barrier leaned away from him, Spike nearly went with it, his gut flipping into his throat at the imagined fall. But he pulled himself back as he watched thirty feet of brick and stone cast a dark shadow over the diseased before crashing down on top of them with an almighty *boom*.

The diseased had wedged themselves so tightly into the alley, it crushed the lot of them. Limbs moved from where many twitched and spasmed.

The shrill cries and hisses had turned into wheezes and pants as Spike shifted back across the ledge to the other wall. A much easier descent compared to the climb, he moved quicker than before.

The wreck of the wall laid out before him, Spike found the largest parts that remained bound together and hopped from one to the other like they were small islands over a sea of diseased.

A wobbly path, but when Spike landed with both feet in the square, he looked back and shook his head to himself. After letting out a relieved laugh, he scanned the plaza for any more of the vile things. If he had to do it all again, he would definitely come up with a different plan. But it had worked. Now he had to find Matilda.

CHAPTER 49

To see the self-imposed grave Spike had slept in sent a slow shudder twisting through his back. How many bugs had he lain with in the night? He snorted an ironic laugh and shook his head. He'd just crushed over one hundred diseased, yet insects still bothered him. After skirting around the small pit and metal sheet, he headed for the city's exit.

The second he stepped from the ruins, Spike saw her. A lump lifted in his throat as he watched her looking back towards Edin, oblivious to his presence. He coughed to allow him to get his words out. "Tilly?"

They rushed towards one another—Matilda moving with a limp—and hugged. Tears ran down Spike's face when he stepped back and looked her up and down. "I've missed you so much. I've been going insane since you disappeared."

Matilda latched on again and squeezed so tightly he almost pulled away from the discomfort of it. "I've missed you too." When she stepped back again, her mouth lifted in a sneer. "I would kiss you, but you look like you've been bathing in their blood."

"I sort of have." With a shake running through him, he shoved a clumsy hand into his pocket and retrieved her hummingbird clip. "Here."

"You found it?"

While taking it from him, Matilda cried harder than before. She stared at the small metal bird in her palm and shook her head. "What have you done?"

"What do you mean?"

"Coming after me."

"What else would I do?"

Matilda regarded him with a hard scowl. "Uh, I dunno … how about *listened* to what I asked you to do? You're supposed to be the next protector."

"But you needed my help. You dropped the clip. You carved hearts into the walls. Who else would be able to follow that trail?"

"I asked you to stay and look after Artan."

"I've listened to a lot of orders over the past few months and followed most of them, many against my better judgement."

"So you know better than me, is that what you're saying?"

"*No.* I'm saying I knew you were alive and needed my help. I knew Artan needed *you* back to help him and I could bring you home. If you didn't want me to find you, why did you carve the hearts?"

"I couldn't shout for help. It's not the best thing to do in a city filled with diseased."

"Who else would have picked up that trail though?"

"But what about the apprenticeship?"

"It's worthless without you. I'd rather know you were alive, even if it means we can't be together."

"And how could you possibly know I was okay?"

"I knew it in my heart. I've ignored my intuition too many times on national service and seen people die who didn't need to. I wasn't going to let that happen to you."

"You could have been wrong."

"But I wasn't."

As much as she looked like she wanted to be angry, Matilda let go of a hard breath, her cheeks puffing. A tremble ran through her words. "It's all gone to shit, hasn't it?"

"Who knows what the future holds?"

While looking back into the ruined city, Matilda said, "If it were just you and me, I wouldn't go back. I hate living in Edin, but—"

"Artan needs you. I get it. Come on." Spike stepped close enough for her to lean on him. "Let's get back to Edin and see what we can salvage from this mess. What happened to your leg anyway?"

"I think it's just a sprained ankle. It's too weak to run from the diseased, but it doesn't feel broken."

After two steps, Spike stubbed his toe, a sharp sting streaking through his left foot. He stopped and pulled the grass to one side to see a sign. It stood just three feet tall and stretched about the same wide. Supported by two metal poles, the wide rectangle had been bleached white by the sun. Were the letters not raised, it would have been illegible. As it was, Spike read the word. "Edinburgh." He pronounced it *Edin-burg*.

"What's Edin-burg?" Matilda said.

"Maybe it's what this ruined city used to be called."

"And why we call ours Edin?"

"I'd guess so."

After letting go of a hard sigh, Matilda said, "How much do you think our leaders aren't telling us?"

Although Spike thought of Mr. P, now didn't seem like the right time. After all, they still needed to live in the place. "I dread to think."

"I *hate* living in Edin. Especially when I think about life after national service."

There seemed little point in agreeing with her. Not that he didn't, but where would it get them? As much as they'd probably be okay outside the walls, it would be a very different existence. Instead of continuing the conversation, Spike said, "Come on, let's go."

∼

Although the day wore on because of their slow return to Edin, Spike and Matilda got to within sight of the new wall without incident. Covered in sweat from supporting Matilda's weight most of the way, Spike scanned for signs of the cadets.

"Do you think they've gone in already?" Matilda said.

Spike squinted against the bright sun and tried to see through the gaps in the walls. When he saw a cadet, he shook his head. "Look, Lance is in there."

"I was kind of hoping he'd have been taken out by now."

"No such luck. He and Ranger will be here at the end." In spite of the regretful twist in his heart, Spike said, "One thing about not doing the trials is I won't have to spend five months living with that moron."

∼

When they stepped inside the wall a few minutes later, Olga shrieked, "You made it!"

The faces of the remaining cadets turned their way. There seemed so few, although from what Spike could see, no one else had fallen.

The loud cry of the team leaders took Spike by surprise, and he stepped back to see Bleach, Juggernaut, and Fright descending on them, weapons raised.

Because Matilda could stand on her own, Spike lifted his

hands in the air, a nervous laugh as he said, "Calm down. We've not been bitten."

"Lie down face first," Bleach said.

"We've *not* been bitten."

"*Lie down!*"

After sharing a glance with Matilda, Spike followed her lead, dropping to his knees before lying face down on the grass.

The three leaders around them, Fright said, "I hope you're telling the truth about not being bitten. We're going to take you two in, strip and shower you, and check your bodies for bites. Until then, we're going to treat you like you're diseased. Now stand up slowly and put your hands behind your back. Any sudden movements and we'll assume you're turning."

Both Spike and Matilda got to their feet. Of all the cadets there, Ranger appeared to be getting the most pleasure from their treatment. Mirth Spike hadn't seen on his face since his trips to the hole, he winked before nudging Lance with his elbow, the pair of them laughing.

When the sharp tip of Fright's sword pressed into his back, Spike stepped towards the gate. Ranger didn't matter one jot at that moment. They had much bigger problems waiting for them.

CHAPTER 50

Other than barked instructions, Bleach ignored Spike. He made him shower, checked his body for bite marks, and gave him some clean and dry clothes. They were now marching from their dorm to the dining hall, the sun setting on the horizon, marking the end of the longest few days of Spike's life.

Bleach stepped aside to let Spike into the hall first, muttering, "It looks like you're going to be spending the rest of your life in the agricultural district."

Although no one had died since he'd been in the ruined city, the place looked empty. Team Minotaur were still strong in number. They all looked at him, as did every other cadet in the place. All except Hugh, who stared off into the middle distance, a glaze covering his brown eyes.

For the briefest moment, Spike and Max shared a look. A tight-lipped smile and a nod of his head, Spike saw Max understood the congratulations for what it was. If Spike couldn't be the next protector, there was no one he hoped to get it more than Max.

Before Spike walked over to his team, Bleach grabbed his arm so hard he winced and dragged in a sharp breath. He turned on his team leader. "Just *tell* me what you want me to do. There's no need to hurt me."

While maintaining his tight grip, Bleach shoved him in the direction of the top table. It took until that moment for Spike to see Matilda sat there, her long brown hair wet from where she'd clearly gone through the same process as him.

The short walk felt like miles as Spike moved towards the stage, his heart galloping from where he felt the attention of every cadet on him. He ascended the four stairs to get to the elevated platform and sat down next to his love. He spoke from the side of his mouth. "What's going on?"

"I don't know. They're pissed though."

"You reckon?"

Sarge stood at the corner of the stage, and like everyone else in the room, he'd watched Spike take his seat. The gesture seemed for effect rather than to serve any purpose, but Spike sat back as their leader hobbled from one side of the stage to the other, his limp slamming a heavy beat against the wooden floor. At the other side, he cleared his throat and addressed the room. "Meet the two biggest idiots of this national service."

The words sent fire racing through Spike. It had been a hard couple of days and he didn't need it. The abuse he could take, but he wouldn't have them talk about Matilda in that way. "How *dare* you call her that!"

Sarge turned on Spike and he noticed Bleach tense in his peripheral vision. "You'd do well to hold your tongue, boy."

The touch of Matilda's hand against his leg helped Spike curtail his response. She spoke beneath her breath. "Leave it. You won't win."

While grinding his jaw, Spike looked at the man.

Sarge grabbed the top of his nose in a pinch and released a sigh. He addressed his feet more than he did the room of cadets, the echo of his voice highlighting just how many were missing.

"There's a little over three weeks of national service left. Try to survive; I'd like there to be at least *one* cadet remaining at the end of this."

As the man left the stage and then the dining hall, the cadets watched on in silence. They were used to his fury, but he'd never looked so dejected.

CHAPTER 51

Spike and Matilda had returned to Edin nearly two weeks previously. In that time, Bleach had continued to only speak to him out of necessity, and Sarge wouldn't even look at them.

Another day outside the wall, Spike took the slow walk with his team to the gates. Since they'd taken in the lady who spoke in a language no one understood, there were more diseased to fight every time they went outside. But it all felt so empty now. Most nights were early; most meals were quiet. While focusing on the gates, lethargy running through him, Spike said, "I just want national service done with now."

Heidi looked across at him. "What will you do after it?"

Until that moment, they'd avoided talking about what would happen next. Part superstition that they wouldn't get there, but mainly because Spike had lost his chance at the trials.

"Look," Max said, "I'm sorry. I've been wanting to say it all along, but I haven't known how. This isn't how I wanted it to turn out."

"You didn't want to be picked for the trials?"

"Not this way, no. Anyway, I *haven't* been picked yet."

"It's just a formality."

After shrugging, Max said, "That may well be the case, but I didn't want it to play out how it has."

Despite the stabbing pain in his chest, Spike nodded at him. "Thank you. I appreciate it."

Hugh had said even less than Bleach over the past few weeks. Since Elizabeth's death, his demeanour had darkened. So when he said, "I'm glad you saved Matilda," it took Spike a few seconds to reply. "Me too. Not that I'll ever see her again after this."

"At least she's still alive." Hugh quickened his pace to get away from the others.

"Hugh, I'm sorry. I didn't—"

Olga placed a gentle hand on Spike's arm. "Let him go. He knows what you meant. Despite all the hours we've spent training together, he still doesn't say any more than a few words to me."

Lethargy running through his blood, Spike's frame sagged with a sigh. "But I didn't mean it like that."

"He knows."

Before anyone else spoke, Bleach caught up to them. "Spike, you're on wall building today."

"*Again?*"

"Did I ask for a debate? You're on wall building. Haven't you killed enough diseased on your heroic mission to save your princess?"

Bleach strode off ahead of them after Hugh, leaving silence in his wake.

∽

One of the hottest summers Spike had lived through, he'd given up wiping his face because his hands were coated in brick dust. Sweat fell from him, his throat parched because his water had run out already. Brick after stone after brick, he built the wall, packing the mixed clay into the gaps.

Hugh made the mixture while Heidi dug. They'd just finished their shift on guard, swapping with Max and Olga. If he couldn't be there himself, Spike would have chosen for those two to be watching his back.

∽

The scream of the diseased rang through the still air. Spike looked to both sides at the other teams, Matilda now with team Chupacabra because the rest of Dragon were dead. They were all ready, but they didn't need to be. The disease burst from the long grass in front of team Minotaur.

Max, Olga, and Bleach drew their swords.

"Let them come to you," Bleach said. The standard advice from every team leader.

Spike stopped building the wall and watched his teammates, his hands twitching with the need to grab his sword. They held their ground like Bleach told them to. Wide and strong stances, they were ready for the fight.

The first of the four reached Bleach. He took it down with both efficiency and power. What had once been a slight woman, he removed its head from its shoulders.

The next one descended on Olga. She swung true, turning her entire body with the slash. Her sword hit the creature at the top of its arm, but her blade came loose in the hilt and bounced off it. Although she moved quickly and turned her sword into a club, the creature moved quicker. It hit her hard and they both fell, Olga's left arm taking the weight of their tumble with a gut-wrenching *crack!*

Before the creature bit Olga, Max lunged at the beast, driving his sword through its temple. But when he pulled back, his blade remained stuck in its head.

On his feet now, Spike drew his sword and looked at the bolt at the top of the hilt. It had been loosened. Hugh then grabbed it from him, twisted the bolt tight, and charged at the diseased with Spike's weapon.

The Hugh before Elizabeth had died had well and truly gone, the waddling boy fearless as he raced into battle.

Bleach took down another diseased while Hugh charged the final one and drove Spike's sword into its face, burying it to the hilt.

As the creature fell back, Spike watched Hugh help Olga to her feet, the fiery girl crying while she held her arm. Hugh said, "I'm sorry. I should have checked the swords this morning."

All the other cadets watched on, especially Ranger. And sure, he could pass his expression off as squinting into the sun, but Spike saw it for what it was. He saw the mirth underlying the twisted scrunch. While pointing at the boy, he shouted, "*He* did this!"

A brick in his hand, Spike sprinted towards Ranger. "You bastard! What are you trying to do? What have Olga and Max ever done to you?"

Before Spike reached Ranger, Juggernaut came from nowhere, knocking him to the ground with a strong arm across his chest.

Bleach caught up to them a second later and pried the brick from Spike's hand. "You need to keep your head, boy."

"Keep my head? Ranger weakened our swords, I *know* he did. All of them were loosened. Who else would it have been?"

All the while, Ranger watched on.

Because both team leaders stood between him and Ranger, Spike could only look at the boy. He'd get him. Whatever it took, he'd get him.

When Heidi screamed, Spike looked away from Magma's son. She stepped back and pointed at Max, who'd lifted his top to reveal a circular wound on his stomach. "He's been bitten! He's been bitten!"

Juggernaut and Bleach raced over to Max, their swords pointed at him.

Tears stood in Bleach's eyes and he breathed quickly. "Is it a bite?"

Max nodded, his shoulders slumping as he looked at the ground.

Bleach yelled as he charged, but Juggernaut grabbed him, dragging him back.

"What are you doing?" Bleach said.

"There's no sign of him turning yet."

"But he will."

"You and I both know that might not be true. With a wound that deep, he should have already gone."

The two men stared at one another before Bleach shook his head and walked away. "He's only a kid. He doesn't deserve this."

CHAPTER 52

A cold chill snaked through Spike as he approached team Phoenix's dorm. It had been left empty since they'd fallen, but they had a need for it now. Although Hugh walked beside him, the once chatty boy didn't speak.

Fright stood guard on the door, waiting for Hugh and Spike to get close enough to hear her. "It's been a long time since we've used a medical centre. In national service, you're usually either healthy or dead."

"I suppose they got lucky, then."

"You think?"

Maybe she knew something he didn't. Either way, Spike pulled a tight-lipped smile at team Chupacabra's leader. Just before he walked into the dorm, he heard his name called and turned around to see Matilda hobbling towards him.

When she caught up, Spike looked down at her bandaged foot. "Still no better, then?"

"They reckon I'm done with national service now. But they won't let me go home until it's over."

"If we do that, sweetie," Fright said, "everyone will be getting themselves injured so they can go home early."

It made sense and Matilda nodded as if to agree with the scary woman. Without another word, the three of them entered the dorm.

Both Max and Olga lay in beds in the same room. They turned to look at them as they entered.

"At least you get to keep each other company," Spike said.

Neither replied.

Before Spike could say anything else, Hugh said, "I'm so sorry. I should have checked the swords."

"*We* should have checked them," Max said. "They were *our* weapons. Besides, we're both okay. You stopped the diseased taking us down. We're both alive and will walk away from this. Please don't blame yourself."

"Blame Ranger," Spike said. "I do."

When Max craned his neck to look at Spike, Spike moved around in front of him to make it easier. "Like I just said to Hugh, we're both still alive. It is what it is, and unless we have concrete evidence that Ranger did this, there's nothing that can be done, and there's no point in going down that path. He's one of the most protected cadets because of who he is. I'm sad this is the end for me—"

"This is the end?" Spike said.

"They said they need to keep me back and do some tests on me. I might hold the key to beating this disease, so I won't be able to compete in the trials. But I had a good life before I came here, and I'm happy to go back to that." While looking from Spike to Matilda, Max's face lit up. "You two have a chance to be together now."

"They won't let me compete," Spike said. "Not after what I've done."

"I think they will. I'm out." Max nodded his head at Olga, her left arm bound and strapped to her. "She's out too. Just make sure you win it, yeah? I expect you to come see me when you have the freedom of the city." He beckoned Spike towards him and they hugged. "Good luck, man."

While Matilda and Hugh said their goodbyes to Max, Spike went to Olga. "It's definitely broken, then?"

She nodded. "I've got to lie here for the next two weeks and wait for this hell to end."

"They said the same to Tilly. At least you can rest. What I'd give to not lift another damn brick again."

"A broken arm?"

"Okay, no, I wouldn't give that. But you didn't want to be in the trials anyway, did you?"

Olga shook her head.

"I'm pleased you're all right."

She smiled. "Me too."

"I'll keep visiting to try to take some of the boredom away."

"Urgh, you'll just make it worse."

The twinkle in her eye made Spike laugh. "I'll see you soon, short arse."

Spike stood at the door, waiting for Hugh and Matilda to speak to Olga before leading them all outside. They were getting towards the end of summer now. A slight chill in the air lifted gooseflesh on Spike's bare arms, but before he could comment on the weather, he saw them.

"Great," Matilda said.

The same familiar twist to his oversized features, Ranger said, "Evening, ladies." He flicked his head in the direction of Phoenix's dorm. "How are your teammates?"

Matilda hobbled closer to the stocky boy. "They're fine. No thanks to you."

"What could you possibly mean, sweetheart?"

"You know what I mean. You messed with their swords like you messed with mine. Like you knocked Elizabeth back so she couldn't run. You might think you've gotten away with it, but you haven't. It'll catch up to you."

In mock surprise, Ranger shrugged. "I genuinely don't know what you're talking about, sweetheart. But if I can help in any way, please let me know. I'd hate to think someone might have put your friends' lives in danger."

Because he'd watched Ranger—studying the smug git for signs of mistruth—Spike hadn't noticed Lance's face. When he saw the boy—puce with mirth and silently laughing at the performance from his friend—heat lifted beneath his collar and he balled his hands into fists. Before he'd given it much thought, Spike lunged at Ranger, fist first, and punched him on his large nose.

Ranger fell back and Spike landed on top of him, sitting on him while raining punches down against his face.

Each blow landed true and with a deep crack. Ranger's fat head snapped from side to side, and he tried to defend against the attack by covering his face with his large hands.

"You're a piece of shit, you know that? You're going to come unstuck, and I'm going to be there to see it." Spike continued to punch the boy, who squealed and yipped from the blows, twisting and turning in a futile attempt to get away.

Two large hands reached under Spike's arms and lifted him off Ranger. He kicked and twisted, fighting to get back at the boy, but he couldn't get free from the restraint. When he heard Bleach's voice, Spike fell limp. "Give it up."

Blood ran from Ranger's nose, and as Lance helped him get to his feet, he wiped it with the back of one hand while pointing at Spike with the other. "*He* needs to go in the hole."

After tossing Spike aside, Bleach stepped close to Ranger. "For what?"

"What do you *mean*? He just attacked me."

A slight frown, Bleach shook his head. "I must have missed

that." Then he turned to Hugh and Liz. "Did you two see anything? I'd hate to call Ranger a liar."

The answer came back in stereo from Spike's two friends. "No."

When he looked at Ranger again, Bleach shrugged. "I don't know what you want me to do? I mean, Spike *might* have attacked you, but I have no evidence to prove it, so there's nothing I can do to help."

The argument contorted Ranger's face and he directed his rage at Bleach. "I'm going to make you pay."

"Is that a threat?" Before Ranger could reply, Bleach said, "Do you need more time in the hole? Maybe a little time to learn how to keep your mouth in check?"

From Ranger's expression, it looked like the retort rose and died in him. He shook his head, spun around, and walked off, Lance jogging to catch up with him.

While watching the pair walk away, Spike said, "Thank you."

"Don't think I approve of what you just did; I just happen to approve of Ranger less."

"You think he tampered with the swords too?"

"Who doesn't?"

"At least Olga and Max are still alive."

"Olga will be fine."

Spike let the silence hang for a second. "And Max?"

Bleach walked back towards their dorm, Spike moving off with him, Hugh and Matilda following behind.

"Juggernaut should have killed the kid."

"How can you say that?"

"I had a brother."

Spike waited for him to say more.

"He got bitten on national service when he was your age. It was thirty-two years ago."

"What happened to him?"

A few seconds of silence, Bleach wincing before he said it. "He died last year."

"So there's hope for Max?"

Bleach stopped and looked at Spike, the green of his eyes glazed and his words catching in his throat. "They kept him locked in a cell from the moment he got bitten to the moment he died. They didn't let anyone visit him. I heard from one of his guards that he lost his mind about fifteen years ago. By the end, he couldn't even remember his own name. He sat in a corner and slammed his head against the wall day and night. But they kept him alive and used his blood to run tests on. His mind didn't matter to them."

"And that's what they have planned for Max?"

"Yep. By saving his life, Juggernaut has just condemned him to something much worse than a sword through the heart."

"We've got to do something."

"What?"

"I dunno, get him out or something?"

Bleach winced as if fighting back tears and nodded over Spike's shoulder. When he spun around to look, he saw five guards from the city leading Max from team Phoenix's dorm. They didn't manhandle him, but he certainly had no choice in the matter. Bleach sighed, his voice breaking. "It's too late for him now."

CHAPTER 53

The start of tears burned Spike's eyes as he stared at the gates, waiting to get back into the national service area for the last time. They were finally done, and now they'd reached the end of their six months, he had nothing left to give.

As he looked to both sides at the cadets who remained, Spike shook his head. Just eleven of them left. Matilda and Olga rested because of their injuries and only the gods knew where Max had been taken. So few to choose from for the apprentice trials, and with Max and Olga down, surely he stood a chance. Not that he would have wanted it this way, but who else would they pick?

The sound of Juggernaut's horn cut through the air, and Spike mirrored those on either side of him by staring at the gates, the muscles in his face slack with exhaustion.

Like when Spike and the others had first arrived for national service, a new batch of rookies were waiting on the other side for their return. Because it was their last day, they were coming home at lunchtime. It gave the new recruits an insight as to what lay ahead. From what Spike could tell, none of the cadets he walked back in with had been bitten while out in the field, so at least they wouldn't have the same introduction he'd had. How many of the new recruits had already failed the idiot test?

When the gates opened, Spike saw a new group of leaders waited with the cadets. He didn't recognise any of them. Although, he didn't make much effort to look, his attention on the ground as he avoided the rookies' loaded stares. If any of them spoke to him, he'd reveal things they didn't need to hear. He'd always been told that if he didn't have anything positive to say, then he shouldn't say anything at all.

But then he heard his name. "Spike?"

Trent from agriculture. The skinny boy stood long and straight. He'd been nicknamed Beanpole. Over six feet tall, he looked like he weighed less than many kids half his height. An awkward mess of angles, the kid was all elbows and knees.

Spike looked at the boy.

"How are you? Have you made the trials? How was it?"

If he couldn't say anything positive ... Spike dropped his focus to the ground and walked past the boy while swallowing against the rising lump in his throat.

Sarge stood in front of the new recruits, so Bleach took control by pointing in the direction of the gym. "We need to head there for our last meal. After that, you're all free to go back to your districts."

∼

AFTER THEIR MEAL OF ROUGH BREAD AND STEW—AGAIN—THE team leaders brought out cake. A plain sponge sweetened with berries, Spike watched the faces of the cadets light up. Because all the tables were in the dining hall, the cadets sat on the floor and ate together. The demarcation lines of team affiliation now gone, Spike sat next to Matilda and Olga. Black and yellow bruising wrapped Matilda's ankle, but she'd managed to put more weight on it with each passing day. As the only member of her team left, she would have gotten into the trials by default, but the injury ruled her out.

The doors to the gym then opened and Sarge strode in, the seven main protectors behind him. They lined up with the remaining team leaders. From left to right, Spike looked along the line: Ore, Flame, Fright, Bleach, Juggernaut, Sarge, Magma, Warrior, Hulk, Axle, Fire, Rayne, Crush.

Sarge stepped from the line, milking the room as he liked to do, walking with his dramatic gait as he hobbled from one side to the other. "For the fallen: You gave yourself in service to this great city. May your spirits watch over us as we grow and prosper. Know we won't forget you when Edin is liberated from the oppressive control of trying to live in a world where the diseased exist. Know you are the reason we'll get there."

When he'd finished, Spike looked at Hugh. Where he expected to see sorrow in his eyes, he saw white-hot fury.

"Now," Sarge said, "you can probably all guess why we're here."

The butterflies in Spike's full stomach sent a twinge of nausea through him. He'd worked so hard to get here. It took all he had to not reach across and hold Matilda's hand. Instead, he looked at the faces of those around him. Many were pale with exhaustion. When he looked at Ranger, he found the boy staring straight back at him. Ranger winked. Did he know something Spike didn't? He looked at Magma and met his hard scowl.

"We've had one team completely wiped out, which means we have no cadets for the trials from team Phoenix. And with Matilda's ankle, Dragon don't have a representative either."

The space where two team leaders should be seemed all the more gaping when Sarge talked about the fallen.

"From team Bigfoot," Sarge sounded apathetic when he read the name, "Ranger Hopkins."

Ranger wore a smug grin while lapping up the applause from his pet, Lance.

"From Chupacabra, we've chosen James Swank. From team Yeti, Fran Jacobs. From team Cyclops, it's Liz Barber. And finally, from Minotaur, Hugh Rodgers."

"What?" Spike said. The room fell silent and turned on him, including Hugh. When he looked at Matilda, he saw tears in her eyes. "Surely I've done enough to be selected?"

Ranger snorted a laugh and Lance joined in.

A red wash to his face, Sarge's voice shook when he said, "You *broke* the rules, William. What do you expect?"

Spike shook his head and stared at the wooden floor, the air ripped from his lungs. He'd given so much, and with Max gone, he had to be the obvious choice. It took all he had, but he turned to Hugh and patted his back. "Well done, mate."

"I'm sorry, man."

"You've nothing to be sorry for."

"Hang on!" Juggernaut stepped from the line of leaders and protectors. "We can't only have five cadets."

"Why not?" Sarge said.

"If we want to give the crowd some entertainment, the more the better, right? Especially as they know seven teams went out. I say we should take at least one more."

"So what, we let someone else in? Someone who hasn't earned it?"

"And that's my other reason for saying this. I think William has earned it."

"*William?*" Both Sarge and Bleach said it in unison.

While shrugging, Juggernaut said, "Yeah. He's been great outside the wall, and the only time he's gone against the rules is to help other people. He's put himself in the firing line from both you and the diseased for the safety of others."

Sarge snarled. "That makes him a liability in my book."

"It makes him a hero in mine."

Silence descended on the hall as the two men stared at one another. Ranger broke it. "You can't do that. He's *ignored* the rules. He's attacked *me* several times. He's a liability, like Sarge said."

It seemed to be the thing that made the difference. His attention on Magma's son, Sarge's eyes narrowed. "Let's have a vote to see if he deserves the final spot."

Ranger said, "I vote no."

"I'm not offering you a vote, *boy*." Turning his back on the cadets and facing the leaders and protectors, Sarge said, "I'll go first. I say no."

Ore stared at Spike like she wanted to murder him. "Yes."

"One apiece, Flame?"

"No."

"Fright?"

"No."

"Three to one, Juggernaut?"

"Yes."

"Warrior?"

"Of course, the kid's a maniac. I like maniacs."

"Three all. Hulk?"

"No."

"Axle?"

"No."

"Five–three."

"Fire?"

"Yes."

"Rayne?"

"Yes"

"Five–five."

"Crush?"

"Yes."

"Five–six."

"Bleach?"

"No."

The cadets gasped and Spike felt his world collapse around him. The man he'd worked so hard for had just sold him up the river and given Magma the decisive vote. He glared at his former team leader, and his former team leader glared back while the rest of the room watched Magma.

Ranger sneered at him. "Tough luck, *William.*"

Sarge turned his palms up to the ceiling and said, "Magma?"

The room fell silent, and for a second Magma said nothing, staring at Spike with the same disdain he'd levelled on him since they'd first made eye contact. Spike should have done more to make it okay between them. But he was Ranger's dad. The guy would hate him no matter what.

The large gymnasium seemed too small to contain Magma's voice. Like trying to bottle thunder. Spike could have sworn the windows shook with his deep baritone. "I wouldn't be here if it wasn't for second chances." Something other than rage swirled through his dark eyes when he looked at Matilda. Sadness ... no, not quite. Gratitude. "Matilda's dad was better than me in every way when we did the trials."

The room turned to Matilda, who now cried freely.

"He was set to be one of the greatest protectors of all time, and he deserved a shot at it. But he injured himself. He twisted his right knee and it's never been the same since. As runner-up to him, I was offered his spot. It's why I fight so hard. I fight for both him and myself when I'm faced with the diseased."

Spike didn't care who watched, he reached over and held Matilda's hand. She squeezed so tightly in return, he nearly let go again.

"I wouldn't be here if it wasn't for second chances, so I say *yes*, let him through."

"*Dad!*" Ranger's whine sounded like that of a child half his age.

Magma didn't look at his boy. Instead, he nodded at Spike. "Good luck." And then to Matilda: "Your dad paid a price I can never compensate him for. I hope William manages to make the most of his opportunity and brings you both happiness."

"*Dad!*" Ranger said again.

For the second time, Magma ignored his son, stepping back in line with the others.

Sarge stepped forward again and looked at Spike. "Seven–six in your favour, young man. It's not a decision I would have made, but I respect the opinions of the protectors and team leaders. You're in." He addressed the entire room when he said, "Now, for everyone here, good luck with your lives as citizens of Edin. The gods know you've earned it. For those of you on the trials, go and get some rest. You have one month off. I look forward to seeing you all fit and healthy in four weeks' time."

Spike hadn't let go of Matilda's hand, and as Sarge led the team leaders and protectors out, he looked across to see her still crying. She smiled through her tears. "We still have a chance."

A second to compose himself, Spike nodded. "I'm going to win the trials. I promise."

END OF BOOK TWO.

Thank you for reading *National Service - Book two of Beyond These Walls*. Book three - *Retribution* is available now at www.michaelrobertson.co.uk

Support the Author

Dear reader, as an independent author I don't have the resources of a huge publisher. If you like my work and would like to see more from me in the future, there are two things you can do to help: leaving a review, and a word-of-mouth referral.

Releasing a book takes many hours and hundreds of dollars. I love to write, and would love to continue to do so. All I ask is that you leave an Amazon review. It shows other readers that you've enjoyed the book and will encourage them to give it a try too. The review can be just one sentence, or as long as you like.

If you've enjoyed Protectors, you may also enjoy my other post-apocalyptic series - The Alpha Plague. Books 1-8 (the complete series) are available now.

The Alpha Plague - Available Now at
www.michaelrobertson.co.uk

Or save money by picking up the entire series box set at
www.michaelrobertson.co.uk

THE ALPHA PLAGUE
THE COMPLETE SERIES
MICHAEL ROBERTSON
THE ALPHA PLAGUE 1
THE ALPHA PLAGUE 2
THE ALPHA PLAGUE 3
THE ALPHA PLAGUE 4
THE ALPHA PLAGUE 5
THE ALPHA PLAGUE 6
THE ALPHA PLAGUE 7
THE ALPHA PLAGUE 8

ABOUT THE AUTHOR

Like most children born in the seventies, Michael grew up with Star Wars in his life. An obsessive watcher of the films, and an avid reader from an early age, he found himself taken over with stories whenever he let his mind wander.

Those stories had to come out.

He hopes you enjoy reading his books as much as he does writing them.

Michael loves to travel when he can. He has a young family, who are his world, and when he's not reading, he enjoys walking so he can dream up more stories.

Contact
www.michaelrobertson.co.uk
subscribers@michaelrobertson.co.uk

ALSO BY MICHAEL ROBERTSON

The Shadow Order

The First Mission - Book Two of The Shadow Order

The Crimson War - Book Three of The Shadow Order

Eradication - Book Four of The Shadow Order

Fugitive - Book Five of The Shadow Order

Enigma - Book Six of The Shadow Order

Prophecy - Book Seven of The Shadow Order

The Faradis - Book Eight of The Shadow Order

The Complete Shadow Order Box Set

∽

The Blind Spot - A Dystopian Cyberpunk Novel - Neon Horizon Book One.

∽

The Alpha Plague: A Post-Apocalyptic Action Thriller

The Alpha Plague 2

The Alpha Plague 3

The Alpha Plague 4

The Alpha Plague 5

The Alpha Plague 6

The Alpha Plague 7

The Alpha Plague 8

The Complete Alpha Plague Box Set

∼

Protectors - Book one of Beyond These Walls
National Service - Book two of Beyond These Walls
Retribution - Book three of Beyond These Walls
Collapse - Book four of Beyond These Walls
Beyond These Walls - Books 1 - 3 Box Set

∼

The Girl in the Woods - A Ghost's Story - Off-Kilter Tales - Book One.

∼

Masked - A Psychological Horror

∼

Crash - A Dark Post-Apocalyptic Tale
Crash II: Highrise Hell
Crash III: There's No Place Like Home
Crash IV: Run Free
Crash V: The Final Showdown

∼

New Reality: Truth
New Reality 2: Justice
New Reality 3: Fear

Printed in Great
Britain
by Amazon